RACE AGAINST TIME

Trey ran down the streets of Avalon, his mind racing ahead of him. He had no one to turn to now. He was going to get no help from the police. They had their own agenda, their own strategy when it came to catching killers like Agnes. It often took days to track down such killers. By then she might have added three more victims to her list. Trey felt a cold sweat break out along his scalp and neck. He had to do something.

Time was running out. His family may have already been killed. But that wasn't what Agnes Hatcher would use them for.

She would use them for drawing him to her.

He wasn't going to let anything happen to his wife and children.

He wasn't going to let them die at the hands of the monster.

He had only himself as a weapon.

But it was his best weapon, because Agnes Hatcher wanted *him* . . .

From the quiet menace of its opening pages to its stunning, nerve-shattering conclusion, BAD KARMA is a novel that rivals those of Jonathan Kellerman and Dean Koontz for sheer terror and suspense. A story in the chilling tradition of FATAL ATTRACTION and CAPE FEAR, BAD KARMA will linger long after you've triple-bolted your doors and turned out the lights . . .

THE ONLY ALTERNATIVE IS ANNIHILATION . . . RICHARD P. HENRICK

SILENT WARRIORS (8217-3026-6, $4.50/$5.50)
The Red Star, Russia's newest, most technologically advanced submarine, outclasses anything in the U.S. fleet. But when the captain opens his sealed orders 24 hours early, he's staggered to read that he's to spearhead a massive nuclear first strike against the Americans!

THE PHOENIX ODYSSEY (0-8217-5016-X, $4.99/$5.99)
All communications to the *USS Phoenix* suddenly and mysteriously vanish. Even the urgent message from the president canceling the War Alert is not received, and in six short hours the *Phoenix* will unleash its nuclear arsenal against the Russian mainland. . . .

COUNTERFORCE (0-8217-5116-6, $5.99/$6.99)
In the silent deep, the chase is on to save a world from destruction. A single Russian submarine moves on a silent and sinister course for the American shores. The men aboard the U.S.S. *Triton* must search for and destroy the Soviet killer submarine as an unsuspecting world race for the apocalypse.

CRY OF THE DEEP (0-8217-5200-6, $5.99/$6.99)
With the Supreme leader of the Soviet Union dead the Kremlin is pointing a collective accusing finger towards the United States. The motherland wants revenge and unless the USS *Swordfish* can stop the Russian *Caspian*, the salvoes of World War Three are a mere heartbeat away!

BENEATH THE SILENT SEA (0-8217-3167X, $4.50/$5.50)
The Red Dragon, Communist China's advanced ballistic missile-carrying submarine embarks on the most sinister mission in human history: to attack the U.S. and Soviet Union simultaneously. Soon, the Russian *Barkal*, with its planned attack on a single U.S. submarine, is about unwittingly to aid in the destruction of all mankind!

Available wherever paperbacks are sold, or order direct from the Publisher. Send cover price plus 50¢ per copy for mailing and handling to Kensington Publishing Corp., Consumer Orders, or call (toll free) 888-345-BOOK, to place your order using Mastercard or Visa. Residents of New York and Tennessee must include sales tax. DO NOT SEND CASH.

BAD KARMA

Andrew Harper

Pinnacle Books
Kensington Publishing Corp.
http://www.pinnaclebooks.com

PINNACLE BOOKS are published by

Kensington Publishing Corp.
850 Third Avenue
New York, NY 10022

First Printing: February, 1998
10 9 8 7 6 5 4 3 2 1

Printed in the United States of America

For John Scognamiglio and Kay McCauley, with thanks.

Special thanks to my unnamed sources regarding the incarceration of the criminally insane as well as to the work of psych techs. Thanks to the Caldwell, California, police department and information services for procedural information. Thanks to Raul Silva, for additional research and development, and to Lisa, Steve, Charlotte, and Cheryl for helping when I was stuck. Final thanks to my parents and my sister for unflagging support and understanding.

Note to the Reader: Both Santa Catalina Island and its town of Avalon exist, and are among the beautiful jewels of the California coast. I dare anyone not to fall in love with that island. However, I have fictionalized both the police force on the island, as well as some topographical irregularities. If there is any resemblance to island residents and/or tourists living or dead in this work of complete fiction, it is purely coincidental. As to the accomplice from the late 1800s, it is highly likely that the legendary mystery had some help in his deeds.

Escape me?
Never—
Beloved!
While I am I and you are you.

Robert Browning, *Life in a Love*

PROLOGUE

The oven was wide and deep. It was used as a furnace for the brothel above when coal could be afforded. The beating at the door was getting louder, and she could hear the dogs barking. She hated the dogs more than anything. Looking up through the grate, she saw the carriage on the cobblestones. Men were looking inside it, as if expecting to find them there.

But someone had seen them come into their nest.

They were at the door.

"You must hide," she whispered, kissing his throat. She wrapped herself up in his cloak. They would think that she was him. She would crawl through the space behind the wall and come out by the river. She could go down through the sewers and wait.

Later, she would come back. She whispered all this to him.

"Promise?" he asked, holding her tight. "You won't abandon me?"

She promised with kisses, and helped him squeeze into the small stone chamber. She took coal and rags and stuffed them up the opening, so he could not be seen.

They were trying to smash the door in, and she heard the horses outside whinnying as if they were being beaten.

She ran over and knelt beside the loose bricks, pulling them out two by two. She was nearly as small as a child, and squeezed herself through, scraping her knees against the ragged stones. Then, snakelike, she slithered through the crawl space, slowly.

She heard the door burst open.

She waited.

The dogs howled and sniffed at the crawl space, but within minutes they left.

The alarm was over.

They hadn't caught him.

Her beloved was safe.

She backed up through the cramped space, to the room.

As she drew herself up and out of the tunnel, her first thought was to go tell him that it was safe. For in that stone chamber where he was hidden, he could not possibly hear anything.

And then she saw the locket.

Pinned inside his cloak.

She opened it up, curious.

She saw what was inside it.

The woman reliving this memory awoke briefly.

She was chained to a bed.

She could see only shadows and light.

She knew she must reach him. She must make things right with him. But she closed her eyes, because she longed to return to that other world.

The world of her nightmares.

PART ONE

CHAPTER 1

He was on the boat when it happened.

Trey Campbell glanced up, thinking he'd heard something, perhaps the cry of a gull. He saw the tall white cliffs to the west of the island, the natural wonder of Catalina. The Kirk in the Rocks, as it was popularly known. Within those cliffs was a series of interconnecting caves and tunnels that he had once believed created a great labyrinth within the island. As a boy he'd scaled those rocks, and explored what seemed then like endless trails through the caverns. His father had taught him to shoot a gun from those cliffs, but not to kill anything. That was forbidden. To shoot bottles and skeet and even as a warning in the air to a trespasser if the situation warranted it. But never at anything that breathed.

A gun firing in the dark morning . . .

He felt a cold sweat break out along his back and neck. Not from the heat, but from what seemed, momentarily, like a primal fear of creation itself: the sea, the rocks, the endless sky. He knew it was irrational, perhaps even a sign of a panic attack. A second later, the world was normal again. Fear was gone. The gun that had accidentally gone off in his remembered dream was silent.

A white flash in a dark room . . .

Later, he'd remember that sense, as if he'd heard a warning shot, but at that moment he was more concerned with his fishing line. He had developed that capacity over the years, to forget painful memory and to attend to what was directly in front of him.

During the three hours out to sea, all that he could possibly fear would come to pass, but from a distance.

For now he could relax and try to enjoy the sea, the air, the boat.

The boat was a Bayrunner Westcoaster, a fourteen-footer, welded marine metal, made for rough weather, but not designed to traverse the twenty-six some miles between San Pedro, on the mainland, and Catalina Island. It was for harbor fishing, the man who rented the boats told him. It would be at anyone's risk to take it out farther than two miles from the island.

He and his wife were barely out a mile in the boat. He wished he could take it out farther, not just for the fishing, but for the peace and calm. The boat was rented for the week, and came with the requisite nicks and dents and a kind of pallor to the metal. The outboard motor was a two-cylinder with thirty-five horsepower, which he'd had a hard time starting. He had killed the motor an hour before, and cast his line down.

His wife, Carly, didn't enjoy fishing but loved being out at sea. She set her paperback down for a moment and scanned the island, as if she'd left something behind there and perhaps wanted to go back for it.

"Water's too warm," he said. "All the squid probably

moved on to colder currents, and all the yellowtail followed, maybe even the white sea bass too. I'll be damned lucky if I catch a halibut."

"Poor baby," Carly said. "We can have yellowtail up at the café without having to put a hook in some fish mouth." She grinned. She found fishing boring, but the sea soothing.

"Ah," he said. "But it's so much better when the fish has a fighting chance. Makes me feel manly to catch it. Makes me feel like Hemingway."

"I didn't know Mariel Hemingway fished," his wife said, flicking water at him. She giggled. "Oh, Trey, so serious with your fishing. You must feel like I'm keeping you chained to my side, just when you're dreaming of freedom on the open waves." She crossed her arms behind her head for support and closed her eyes against the sun. "How awful to have a wife like me. Well, it's only a few years to your mid-life crisis. Then you can chase blondes, drive little red Miatas, and comb your hair over whatever bald spot's going to emerge between now and fifty."

He shook his head, grinning. "Chained and happy. Just wish I could go back . . . stop things before they happened . . ." He couldn't look at his wife then.

"Stop it," Carly said tenderly. She sat up again, returning her attention to her paperback.

"Romance?" he asked.

"Hardly. It's the story of a guy who goes with his wife on vacation and manages to make the whole trip as stressful as possible until the wife has no choice but to run off with the cabana boy."

The sea was a sheet of brilliant cobalt, the sky was bone white, the boat was gently rocking. He did most of his fishing near the rocks, just beyond the breakwater. Carly had insisted on bringing a cooler full of sodas, and he knew that it would be a problem later. He watched her, now, as she drank a Pepsi, her hair dark and shiny beneath his old San Diego Padres baseball cap, which was to keep the sun off her face—at thirty, she was becoming slightly worried about having spent her entire life at the beach down in San Diego, worried less out of vanity, more out of fear of the skin cancer that had weakened her father before his death.

But she was so far away from death—that's what he thought then. She still looked as she had at twenty as far as he was concerned, although she claimed she was getting fat. Actually, truth be known, he was putting on a bit of a paunch which he was trying to fend off with an exercise routine, because he just couldn't give up the twice-weekly trips to Baskin-Robbins for banana splits. He was just thirty-six, jogged four miles three times a week, and swam a mile or two at the local gym whenever he thought of it. He had been an unathletic child, but for some reason, in his late twenties had begun a regimen that allowed him a few beers and some ice cream. One thing he couldn't stand to do were sit-ups, or what were now called crunches, and, thus, the paunch.

These were his thoughts as he sat in the small boat, clutching his Penn 850 SS rod, praying for a nice fat fish. There was the one thought that had plagued him for the past year, finally driving him to take this vacation, perhaps even quit his job. He kept that thought a secret, buried deep within him most of the time. He could forget about it for now. *Catalina. The Pacific. Sun.* So far removed from his nightmares. The island so close, and yet far enough away that no sounds could be heard from the tourists onshore. He was soaking it in: the cool spray of mist as the boat rocked. The flatness of the light across the water. The heat at the back of his neck from the sun. The feeling that one of his legs had fallen asleep. The first twenty-four hours on Catalina had been spent recovering from the stress of work, the next twenty-four in just wanting to get out of bed and do something.

And now he wished things could always be the way they were, right at that moment.

Right now.

How beautiful his wife was to him, with her dark skin and her Latin eyes. And how much she had taught him in their fourteen years together, through the fights and the trials, how things had worked out as if they'd been meant to.

There was a loveliness in her he could not find when he looked at other women. It went further than flesh and bone. It was some spark within her. He grinned as he watched her. She was everything to him sometimes. Before he'd met her, he had been stupid, a clod, someone who was destined to muddle through life uneventfully. After meeting her, well, to him at least, it had been like a magical transformation. Love itself had become the most powerful transformer he had ever encountered. He knew of men who took their wives for granted, but he was not one of them.

"Trey," she said, calling him by his family nickname. "Trey?"

He leaned toward her, because apparently she was about to tell him a secret.

She whispered, "I got to go, sweetie. Right now."

"So ladylike."

"I thought so."

"I told you not to bring so many sodas," he sighed.

"I know. Why is this such a problem? You haven't exactly been reeling them in." She half grinned. "Besides, you guys have it easy. You can just hang it off the side of the boat. I'd have to lean over the edge and probably capsize the whole thing." Then she gripped his hand and said almost sternly, "I *really* have to go."

Starting the motor was difficult. He had to put all his weight into it, pushing his feet against the transom as he pulled on the rope. The boat rocked less gently. Carly clung to the sides of it. Finally, he got it going and steered toward shore.

It took half an hour to bring the boat back into the dock. It was early in the day, so the tourist boats were still circling around Avalon. He had to maneuver his small fishing boat around to the side of the docks and then kill the motor and row in. As soon as they pulled beside one of the low docks, Carly practically leapt off the boat, leaving him rocking. She ran in her bathing suit, towel around her waist, carryall slung over her shoulder, toward the rest rooms.

He wiped his forehead—it was going to be a hot day—and grabbed a Dr Pepper out of the cooler. His nickname, Trey, came because, as the oldest son in his family, he was named William Campbell the Third, or *tres* in Spanish, which became anglicized. So he had been dubbed Trey—but only his closest friends and family used this name for him. Most of his coworkers knew him as Billy Campbell.

Work was a different identity in more than name alone. He never thought about it when he was home, or on vacation (like this particular week). He had always hoped to get into another line of work, but now, after fourteen years, he could do his job by rote. His and Carly's incomes combined were enough to make them more than comfortable. He wasn't even sure he could do anything else for a living—it wasn't as though he were a doctor, or even a therapist—he was a psych tech, a supervisor, and even though it was a secure position, he had never, when he got into it in his early twenties, expected to make it a career. He'd intended to go on and get a master's and maybe become a therapist, but then Teresa had been born, and then Mark, and Carly was actually able to go on and finish her master's . . . and then the money and security at Darden State became so good, how could he walk away from that? With kids and a life, how could he make a change without disrupting the entire flow of the world?

But now he was considering quitting his job to start over because the stress had really gotten to him with recent events. Carly was making enough to cover for both of them if they drew their belts in tight. He could maybe go back for that graduate degree. . . . In these seven days on Catalina, he was going to figure out what the hell he was going to do with the rest of his life. His dream was to live in a Jimmy Buffet song and bum around on islands like this one to the end of his days. He knew this wasn't the most practical of plans, and would definitely not put Mark and Teresa through Stanford in the future. Neither would that plan entirely wash with Carly.

But, he thought, looking over at the old casino and the hills beyond it, as another magnificent day unfolded in Avalon, wouldn't it be nice? No more Darden State, no more fears, no more stress, no more nightmares about the more extreme patients coming for me. No more remembering Jo-Jo ripping his genitals off with his hands, or of Lorena Davis, naked and drenched in her own blood, using the broken-off fluorescent rod as a weapon, jabbing at him. These were the basics of Darden State, and that word that dare not speak its name in these politically correct times: Insane.

And the shadow against the dark morning as it became visible with the white flash of gunshot.

As if the word "fear" could be written with light against darkness.

His beeper began vibrating in his shirt pocket.

"Dammit," he muttered, knowing it was some emergency from work that he probably didn't even need to know about. He couldn't leave Darden State for even three days before Jim Anderson messed up and gave the wrong meds to the wrong patient.

At least, he hoped it was something that simple.

Later, he would remember how innocent things were just a moment before he made that phone call.

Later, he would remember even the smell of the sea, wood-rotted and fishy, as part of a wonderful innocence that would never again exist for him.

CHAPTER 2

The Darden State Hospital for the Criminally Insane takes up twenty-three acres, and has its own post office. So, officially, it is located in Darden, California, although the town that encircles it is called Caldwell. It is in Riverside County, just northeast of Moreno Valley, in a large canyon between two ridges. Its chain-link fences are twenty feet high, and, at the top, encircled with coiled razor wire. Within the tall outer fence there is a shorter fence, less than ten feet high, which carries a thin electric current, enough to stun a human being for several minutes. Twenty years ago it had only one high fence, but every once in a while a patient escaped. The town of Caldwell was none too appreciative of hearing the lone siren, a leftover from air-raid days, after midnight, signaling that one of Darden's finest was on the run.

The history of Darden is the history of America's attitude toward both criminals and mental illness. The hospital was built in the 1890s, and originally was completely underground. In those days, a paranoid schizophrenic who had murdered or committed some antisocial crime was treated worse than an animal—chained to a wall, food pushed with a stick through the slot in the door. The underground chambers prohibited escapes, and the community at large did not have to be reminded of the hospital's existence. There were fewer than ten percent of the patients with a history of criminal activity; many of them were alcoholics and drug addicts who were placed there by loving families.

Darden remained underground until just after World War II, when it became a center for lobotomies and radical treatments, ice baths, shock treatments—one doctor used to walk room to room, and randomly shock patients whenever the mood took him. Sometimes it was the best treatment available.

The patients who arrived at Darden began to come by way of the criminal justice system, a famous court in Los Angeles, 95-A, which was also known as the Zoo because of the outbursts from those suffering from psychotic rages during their hearings. With this new class of patient, Darden became known as the Crackup Palace, a joking reference to the comparative luxury with which some of its patient-inmates lived. There were escapes occasionally, reaching an all-time peak of three a year within two decades.

In the 1960s, with the availability and research with psychotropic drugs, pills became the favorite candies of Darden. The ten- and fifteen-foot-high fences went up, and the nearly constant escapes dropped dramatically with the constant sedation of the more dangerous patients, and with a more recreational approach to patient care. The Darden patient now wears an orange Darden T-shirt, and has calisthenics in the morning, recreational therapy in the afternoon, can call friends collect, can accept calls and money from outsiders. Occasionally, if they were sneaky enough, the patients can even make love, as the hospital is not only made up of both male and female patients, but they are allowed to intermingle freely at certain times of the day. The belief is that the various meds that each patient ingests keep them far enough away from his or her true feelings so as to be safe.

But even passion cannot be drugged or shocked from a man's system.

It was at five A.M. that Rob Fallon glanced down the hallway to see if the night-shift whore was still in the hallway.

His roommate slept on, snoring every now and then to punctuate the delicious silence of dawn. Rob loved that hour. That moment. It was as if the entire ward were drugged and groggy, and no one, not even the orderlies, could think clearly so early in the day.

It was two hours before the night-shift personnel went home.

Ten minutes before the night-shift whore walked down the hallway. Her shoes tapping the newly waxed floor. Her heavy orthopedic shoes. *Her fat ankles. Her smell. Her taste.*

The corridors gleamed in the long stretch of fluorescent lights from above. It was a green glow, from the recent paint job, done, Rob knew, because the state inspector would be coming in a week. There was a grapevine among the patients, and someone at Patton State, over in San Bernardino, had come to Darden for some tests, and mentioned the inspector's visit there. *So that's why the flowers were planted out on the edge of the baseball field, and that's why the kitchen smelled of bleach and that's why Dr. Wijiwardene was conducting physical evaluations all month long.*

The why of things was very important to Rob. He had been taught about the why of things early in life by his mother. Her why was to create him. That was her sole reason for existence. His mother taught him all the ways. She was a brilliant woman, but ultimately she had outlived her why. All women did.

He had a why: He was a child of God, and that was why he was on earth, to just be. That was his why. He was a young man—twenty-six—who had a genius I.Q. Under different circumstances (he thought) might have been a world leader or a brilliant poet. Instead, he had murdered three of his girlfriends, keeping their heads in water in his kitchen sink. The sink was large, the industrial kind. It could've fit a few more heads, but Rob had been arrested before he could collect another one. The heads still spoke to him when he was by himself, and they told him about all the secrets of the world. They told him about the whys. He told the policeman who arrested him that just because he cut off their heads didn't mean they had stopped living. They were still there, hiding from him, talking to him, telling him that they loved him. The heads.

Rob tried to show remorse for his crimes, but he didn't really understand remorse, or guilt, or shame. Still, he was very good at convincing women that he wallowed in misery and pain.

And he was one of the most beautiful creatures in all of creation. He had been told so on countless occasions throughout his life. He was an Adonis from his earliest years, and women had always loved him. *Always.*

That was why the night-shift whore was in love with

him. That was her why—with women, he knew, the why usually had to do with love.

Donna Howe.

She was ugly, a dog's dog, a two-bagger hump. She had a nose like a potato, and skin scarred and mottled with pits and craters. She was six foot two, broad shoulders, no boobs, a rear end like two old sagging pumpkins left out too long after Halloween. She'd remained a virgin till she was forty-one, which is when Rob first did her. She was a beast on the outside, but a total romantic within. She was meant to be used. She was meant to be taken by him.

Six weeks ago.

She had been easy to seduce. She had never had a date, and Rob looked like a hunk, he knew it. He knew how to get a girl to like him, any girl. He could've written a book on it: *You just find out what they like in a guy, and then you become that thing, that guy, that dream.*

It was always so easy for him.

It was time, now, for her weekly dose of his lust, so Rob gave a whispery whistle, knowing that the night-shift whore would be waiting, listening just for this sound. She had never had it so good, he knew, and she was just about at the point when she would do anything for him.

He didn't plan on killing her.

He didn't consider himself a killer. He had never killed anyone. He had cut off his girlfriends' heads, but it hadn't killed them. They had kept talking, telling him about the men their bodies were still humping, all the tens of thousands of men who were laying them, even now, humping them all over, every orifice they had, and then some. *Humping. Doing. Making.* He couldn't say the F word, just like he couldn't say the V word. He couldn't even think them. He had used those words only once in his life. Never again. He had learned not to use them from the scrubbing that his mother had given him. He had learned never ever ever to use the F or V words again. He had felt the wire brushes against his skin. *The Comet. The Clorox. The rubbing alcohol.* His mother could not get him clean enough after he had said that F word. She spent half the night trying to, but she could not wipe it off his skin, his face, his tongue.

And the V word. His mother had told him to call it a purse. *"It opens up like a purse," she told him. "It's where you put all the things you don't want anyone to see."*

He was a nice boy. His mother had raised him to be a nice boy.

How could a boy like him kill anyone?

Rob Fallon did not plan on killing the night-shift whore.

He could never do a thing like that.

But he did need her eyes.

He did need her eyes.

Then he would see her why.

Her why was in the eyes.

CHAPTER 3

"Hey," Rob Fallon said casually. He leaned against the door frame. He could be James Dean if he wanted. He was as cool as anyone could be. He flashed a grin.

The woman wearing the white and blue uniform was moving slowly. She held a chart in her hand, close to her small breasts. She wore too much makeup. Her eyes were blue smudges. Her lips were crimson.

Rob could tell just by the way she moved that she had begun getting frightened of him. She was like a rat standing before a snake. She stopped in the hallway and leaned against the wall.

She stared at him.

In her eyes, that look of fear.

He would have to calm her.

He drew a folded piece of paper from his back pocket. He held it up. "I wrote this for you."

Her fear seemed to retreat. Her squinty eyes cleared. She was a girl in love. She was his.

She glanced up and down the hall. There was the distant echo of the cooks in the cafeteria as they clanged plates and trays and metal utensils.

No other sound.

Her heavy footsteps. Her fat ankles. Her uniform, so unbecoming on her unwieldy form.

The night-shift whore stepped over to the doorway.

Rob Fallon handed her the note.

She unfolded the lined notebook paper. She read the poem. She half grinned.

He watched her eyes. No fear there. They were bloodshot. They were small. Lurking within them, her *why*.

"It's beautiful," she whispered, looking over his shoulder at his roommate. "You wrote this?"

"Yeah," he said, and believed it himself, even though he'd copied it out of one of the books in the library. But Rob believed that he was the author of all.

He leaned forward and kissed her on the lips, slipping his tongue into her mouth. She accepted it, and he reached for her, holding her. When he withdrew from her lips, he whispered, "I've wanted you for so long. Just for a kiss. Nothing but a kiss. We don't have to do what we did before. I know it was wrong."

"I can't," she whispered, shrugging off his embrace, stepping back. "It's too risky. When you're released, we can be together. It's too dangerous now."

He sighed. "I know. I think about you all the time. I think about our life together. How I want to be with a woman like you, someone who loves and accepts love. I wish . . . I wish things could be different."

An expression of sadness etched across her face. "I wish life were easier."

Rob Fallon nodded. He leaned against her again, took her head in his hands, pressed her lips against his. He slid his lips across her face to her cheek, then her nose, then to her left eye.

He kissed her eyelid.

Something in him urged: *now.*

The why is in her eyes.

He tasted her eyelid. Salty. Bitter from the blue eyeshadow.

She whispered, "Do you love me?"

He kissed from her eyelid to her forehead to the edge of her scalp down to her ear. He whispered, "Yes. God, yes."

He felt the rhythm of her body, something beyond her control as it pressed against his. He knew that that place between her legs, her purse, was opening for him. He knew that her purse wanted him inside her.

He whispered, "Where can we go? I need you now. Right now."

CHAPTER 4

Another patient, two doors down from Rob Fallon's room, on the other side of steel double doors, stirred in her sleep. The room was practically bare. A single chair in the corner, beneath the barred window, which was shuttered also. The bed itself, a narrow hospital bed with criblike bars along one side. The blankets were olive drab, the woman's skin, where her hand showed, was pale white. Her hand twitched slightly.

She was dreaming: *The gleaming metal in her hands, and looking into her lover's eyes as they shared this most secret of pleasures. The yellow flickering glow from the candles. The smell of animal fat as it cooked in the large pot set down in the hearth. The sounds of the street, beyond the cramped stone basement—horses on cobblestones, the cry of a fishmonger, the shouts as the copper from around the corner came upon some creature dying in an alleyway.*

But in their sanctuary, the man and woman, caressing each other.

The tastes between their lips, mingling.

She had a thin cloth over her face, almost like a pillowcase but lighter, like a thin gauze. Still, breathing was easy. She could see shadow, but only during the daytime, if they unshuttered the windows. She didn't mind the cloth too much. It was supposed to be removed at night, but sometimes they forgot. Sometimes they left it on because they didn't want to see the face beneath it. Sometimes she wished she could scrape that face away herself. She wished she could find her true face beneath this one, the one that was lurking. The face that had no skin.

Her arms were strapped to the sides of the bed. Her feet were similarly strapped. Her fingers were strapped too, as if someone thought that if even one of those fingers were loose, it would be too dangerous.

That even a single finger might mean that this small, pale woman might tear her way out of her tether and claw her way through wall and flesh for release from this place. She was small—barely five foot one, and built proportionately, like a doll, perfect hands, perfect waist, perfect legs, perfect hips. Her hair was long and blond. It needed cutting, but sometimes they forgot to attend to this detail. Her skin had chafed some, and she had bedsores at times. They didn't even always have the decency to turn her over. They used to, but they were getting negligent. She longed to feel sunlight on her face again, to walk in the garden, to talk to the one she had lost, the one who was so close to her and far away at the same time. . . .

A single shaft of light penetrated the room—it was the light from the hallway as someone opened the double doors.

Opening the door to her room too. The metallic scrape of the door as it slid open. The smell of the hallway—rubbing alcohol, a fresh coat of paint, the distant steam of food cooking in the cafeteria.

The woman in the bed began breathing more quietly.

She felt the light across her face.

It was warm.

She was sensitive to these things now.

Time and space, all at once.

She smelled perfume, light, almost undetectable.

Backward and forward, one existence to the next.

She smelled someone's underwear—it was filthy.

The smells pleased her. She was too used to the stink of the putrid food, the odor of rubbing alcohol and the plastic taste of the red and green pills they shoved down her throat.

A woman had come into her room. The womansmell was always the strongest, the most disgusting. This woman was just finishing her menstrual cycle. This woman entering her room had that last scent of dead blood there between her legs. Who else? There were other footsteps.

All right. And a man too.

Good.

The man was very clean. He smelled like Ivory soap. He smelled like—*Johnson's Baby Shampoo? No, something cheaper. A generic brand. Maybe from PayLess, or . . . no,* she couldn't tell. He smelled too clean for someone at this time of the morning. He was someone who kept himself brilliantly clean. Someone who was terrified of filth on himself.

She knew this man. She didn't know him by name, but she knew him by smell. She remembered all, for all she had now were memories. She had a photographic mind, she memorized details and faces and smells and tastes. She had smelled the man once before, passing by her room. He was allowed free rein, she supposed.

He was not like her. He was stupid. Men tended to be stupid, to underestimate others. To assume that women didn't have minds. Men thought women couldn't be doctors, could be only nurses, or orderlies; men thought women should stay home and care for their old people who vomit and urinate all over and stink the place up.

That was what men thought.

But she liked clean men, like this man in her room, with this woman. The woman was dirty—she had to wear an old Elizabeth Arden perfume called Chlöe, the woman in her room did, to cover up the stink of her panties. Her hair smelled greasy too. She washed it only once a week. She kept it in a net, probably, beneath one of those tacky white fake nurse caps.

When men were clean they didn't think, they just were.

But the woman who was walking near her bed now, she smelled like she never douched. *Is the man putting his clean fingers up into the filthy woman's panties?*

The woman in bed held her breath so that she wouldn't have to smell what these intruders in her room were about to do.

They were going to do the most repulsive surgery right there. *Right in my room,* she thought, *and I am chained down, like an animal, I can't do anything about these awful people, how that man is going to get his thing all disgusting with that woman's swampy juices.*

The man moaned a little. He whispered, "She can't hear us, can she?"

The woman giggled. "Honey, she's got so many pills in her, even if she could, she'd never understand it. It'll be better doing it here than in the broom closet. And hell, even if she understands, who'd she tell? She never talks. She's just a thing."

The woman in bed almost giggled too. She wanted

to tell them that she could understand what the clean man was doing to the toad.

She wished the clean man would take this filthy woman into the shower—

sprays of clear, pure water—

and clean her off, make her all clean again.

the robe of red with blood roses sewn across it—

"Robby," the filthy woman said, "I want you inside me now. Please." By the voice, she recognized the woman.

Donna Howe. Just forty-one years old. Single. Bad habits. Bad teeth. Born in Oxnard. Parents in the navy. Lives with two roommates in Moreno Valley, near the mall. Very needy. Large feet.

That was all the information she had on Donna. It was hard to find out about people in Darden, because once you asked someone a few questions, they became cautious.

The man was Robert Fallon. She knew all about him. He was a talker, and very nice, but since she'd been unstrapped for only a few months when she'd first arrived, she had not kept up with him.

Of course, he was insane, and not to be trusted, but he was a bit of a lapdog, so she didn't think he'd be too much trouble. He was a sociopath, she knew, by the standards of psychiatry.

She was not. She knew what she was herself, what her life was all about. But she recognized sociopaths as brothers and sisters, people who had purpose to their lives, and an understanding of the Godlike nature of man that was denied by the other animals. When she had been free to roam, when she had been able to look the other patients in the eye, she could see who was one of her kind. They were a different species from the rest of the world. They were the hunters and the gods of creation. In times past, she or this man Rob might've been the leaders of the animals. Instead, they were cast into prisons and tortured for their superiority. But the woman restrained in bed knew that the true measure of civilization was in how a culture treated her species. *The hunters of men.*

These thoughts didn't erase fear from her mind, however. She still knew that the animals like this woman could hurt her. She knew that this woman was the enemy.

And what if no one came in and saw what these two were doing near her bed? What if they did something to her?

Oh, Lord, the woman in bed thought, *they are animals, they are lower than animals, they are trying to make me do it too, I just know they are, they can't help themselves, oh, why doesn't someone help me, why doesn't someone come through that door and help me? These horrible animals are in my room!*

The man was standing up and doing it to the filthy woman.

Like dogs, oh, someone come in and stop them!

They needed a shower, a warm, wet shower, with someone to scrub them down, to clean them, to sponge off the filth and muck.

The filthy woman was leaning forward. The woman in bed could smell her coffee-stained breath. The filthy woman set her hand down on the edge of the bed, near the straps.

Oh, please, someone help me. There are obscenities in my room.

And then a miracle seemed to happen for the woman in bed, for she was able to draw her index finger and her thumb out from the strap. The filthy woman's slapping hand had loosened it.

Two fingers.

The woman in bed twitched her fingers, restoring

circulation as the disgusting animals pounded against each other.

She touched the tip of her finger to the tip of her thumb.

Freedom.

It was all she needed.

CHAPTER 5

It took the restrained woman ten minutes to get her hand loose and slip it beneath the covers so the animals couldn't see that she was loosening her other hand from the strap. She would not be able to get her feet free, not right away, but she could grab Donna Howe and scrape her face clean before the toad woman would know what hit her.

She doubted that Rob Fallon would mind.

He might be scared of her, but fear was good.

Slowly, carefully, both hands free, the woman in the bed reached up to pull the cloth from her face, the cloth that kept the others from looking at her, from seeing her as a woman.

They wanted to see everyone as animals.

But it was them.

They were the animals.

The woman in bed unveiled her face and wanted to

say "Boo!" to Donna Howe, but when she saw Donna's face, she could only giggle.

Donna's face was covered with sweat. She was being taken like a dog from behind. Her eyes were glazed over from the barbaric act. Donna barely noticed her, as if she were just waking from a dream. Then, when she did notice her, Donna's eyes went wide, and her mouth began to open.

But the woman in the bed grabbed Donna's head by the ears and yanked it down to the bed, next to her own face.

As the woman in bed went to work, the man behind Donna kept pounding his body against hers, his moans becoming louder.

CHAPTER 6

MEMORY: *the room off the alley, near the river, by the bridge. It smelled of rats, and only had a half-dozen candles for light. They flickered yellow and green against the peeling paint of the plaster wall. Water dripped slowly from the ceiling, some of it striking her on the head. But she didn't move, as much out of fear as of lack of will. She could hear the women on the street, hawking their wares to the men. She could hear the creak of wheels as the carts went by. Her skin felt cold. Her blood, warm.*

He had set his hat down on the chair and taken his cloak off too. Beneath it, he wore a fresh white shirt and the finest black trousers. He was a true gentleman.

He said, "I saw it in you, girl. You liked what I did. You loved it, pet, didn't you?"

She nodded, still shivering. She could taste blood in the back of her throat.

"We are alike, you and I. We are of the same mettle. We've known each other before, isn't that true? Not in some wretched

heaven or hell, but in eternity. We are soul mates, child." His eyes were like diamonds—hard and sparkling all at once. "I brought you a gift."

He reached into his black bag and withdrew something covered in a monogrammed handkerchief. Blood had soaked through the silk. "It's something quite beautiful, if you have the talent for seeing beauty. Do you? Do you, my raggedly little urchin?"

She leaned forward.

"Do you love what's on the inside instead of what's on the surface? What is beneath the skin is the truth of our beings. Here is her truth," he said, squatting down beside her, taking her small hand, drawing her to her feet. She was shivering. He wrapped his arm around her and held the thing in the handkerchief up to her face. "It was the part of her where she lived. It was her secret place. Isn't it beautiful?"

She looked on as he unfolded the corners of the handkerchief. When she saw what was within it, she looked away for a moment, because it was the part that she hated the most. She glanced about the room, trying to look at everything but what was in his hand.

She saw herself suddenly in the reflection of the mirror on the wall.

Her face scarred and hideous.

"You are beautiful to me," he said, kissing each one of the incisions on her face.

Someone was screaming out in the street.

She felt lightning burst through her.

Agnes Hatcher awoke in the bed in the last years of the twentieth century.

Her face was covered with blood.

CHAPTER 7

Jim Anderson should've arrived at work between six and six-thirty, but because his Chevy truck was running poorly, his brakes about to give out, he decided to get there at quarter of and avoid traffic. It was still dark out, and he was sleepy. He'd been subbing for Billy Campbell all week, who, the lucky stiff, was vacationing on Catalina. But Jim wanted his three-to-midnight shift back. He wasn't a morning person. The mornings were a pain in the butt, all the patients getting wild when they first woke up, the meds having worn off. At night, at least after supper, they tended to watch TV or read or play board games. Only occasionally, when a television game show like *Jeopardy!* got too exciting, did a riot break out. Even then they weren't that hard to subdue—a little force and a few more pills.

When Jim Anderson got past security and had made it halfway down the hall in Building D, he knew something was different. Not in the usual way of some patient getting in bed with another, or some wild person trying to use one of the fluorescent bulbs as a weapon.

It was a stillness that he had not expected.

A quiet.

Sure, he was early.

Sure, he still wasn't all that familiar with the morning and its routines.

But Donna was not at her desk—and Rita Paulsen hadn't come in yet to relieve her.

Donna's desk was piled with papers and Twinkie wrappers. Although he knew that Donna was fairly disorganized, usually by dawn she would have cleaned her desk off for the next shift.

He looked into a couple of the rooms, but the inmates were still asleep.

The one he had never liked, never enjoyed being around—her room was just through the double doors.

He never looked there.

That woman scared him.

Agnes Hatcher. How she memorized faces and people, and anyone who had ever done her even the slightest harm. She was forty-two, but looked like she was twenty, small, petite, almost girlish. And yet she was a tiger. She was the only patient in D that had to be restrained and covered except at mealtime. And even then they spoon-fed her with a very long spoon. She was in, as far as he could tell, for stalking and planning the killings of four cops, each of whom, she felt, had been rough with her when she'd been arrested for a double murder. Jim didn't know everything about her—he had only seen her picture and had never seen beneath the sack they put over her face—but he knew she was nothing but a destructive force in a human body.

And he stayed away from her.

Jim turned his back on the steel doors.

He shivered. He wasn't going to go through them and check on Agnes Hatcher at six in the morning with no one else around.

And then he noticed a door slightly ajar.

Robby-boy's room.

Rob was okay, a mild-mannered sociopath who had a thing for girls' heads but was fairly easy to control. Like all good sociopaths, Rob aimed to please, at least to Jim's face—and that was all he cared about on the job.

Maybe Donna's there.

Rumor was that Donna had a thing for Rob. It was not unusual for psych techs and orderlies to start having feelings for some of the patients, but it could get out of hand and cross boundaries—and that's when it got dangerous. Jim shook his head: *Darden State is another world.* One of the patients, Crackers, had even told Jim that now that they were friends, it was okay for Jim to screw his colostomy hole, and then Crackers had proceeded to poke at it with his own fingers.

Another world, all right.

Jim decided to go get a cup of coffee before checking on Rob Fallon. It was Campbell's shift anyway—*why should I put myself out this week?*

He went down to the vending machines in the staff room. One of the lazier employees, Soderbergh, was napping on the couch. Jim poked at him with his finger. Soderbergh snarfled away and opened his eyes halfway, as if he were undecided as to whether to fully wake up.

"Where's Donna?" Jim asked as he stepped up to the coffee machine. He dropped fifty cents in and pressed the cream and sugar buttons. He looked back at Soderbergh. "Get up, will you?"

Soderbergh slowly sat up, shaking his head free of sleep. "Huh?"

"Donna. I didn't see her at her desk. She around?"

Soderbergh shrugged. "I saw her a little while ago. What time's it?"

Jim Anderson glanced at his watch. "Six-ten." He reached into the machine and withdrew the small cup of coffee.

"I don't know how you drink that stuff, man," Soderbergh said. "It'll kill you."

"What about Donna?"

"I told you, she's around. She was just in here a while ago. I was snoozing, but I saw her go by in the hall. She'd already changed out of her uniform."

Jim took a sip of coffee. "You don't think she's down there with Fallon again?"

Soderbergh half grinned. "Maybe. He's been sending her love notes."

Jim Anderson shook his head. "Jesus. I knew she was wrong for this ward. I knew it."

"Want me to go see if she's there?"

"No. I'll go. I just hope if she is there, she's giving him meds. I've seen him try this before. I was hoping Donna wouldn't fall for it. What a life, huh?" Jim finished his coffee, tossed the cup in the trash, and headed out of the room.

CHAPTER 8

Walking down the corridor, back to Rob Fallon's room, Jim Anderson checked the other rooms briefly. There were fourteen inmates on D, all fairly docile, owing to the medications each received. But of them, five were considered sociopaths, and the rest had murdered enough people to fill a house. Most of them were still sleeping. A few were sitting up in bed, either just staring out in space, or reading, or playing cards. They had that glassy look in their eyes, of Thorazine and Doltrynol. He nodded to those who were up.

When he got to Fallon's room, the smell of Lysol was overpowering. That cold chill that Jim felt whenever he went into one of their rooms—he felt it, like ice. He never knew if it was him, or them. All he knew was that he felt it.

Sometimes, in the morning, Rob Fallon would be at his table, drawing cartoons on construction paper. Rob was quite a good cartoonist, actually. When he'd been on the outside, Rob had had jobs drawing funny portraits at amusement parks, and made a decent living at it. Jim had one of his cartoons on his refrigerator at home—it was a caricature of Jim in profile, with a question mark over his head, and the word "why" written at the bottom.

But this morning the table was bare. Through the bars at the window the first feeble rays of sunlight speared across the darkness of the room.

Jim flicked on the light to see better.

He heard whimpering, and saw Rob there, hunkered down on the floor in the corner, shivering. He kept his hands clenched shut. He was naked except for a towel around his waist. Jim glanced toward the sink—it was full of dirty brown water. Rob, who liked to be squeaky clean, had been giving himself a sponge bath.

"Rob? You okay?"

Rob didn't respond.

Other smells, beneath the Lysol layer: some kind of bleach.

Fallon cleaned himself and his surroundings incessantly. He could've gotten the brand-name cleaners from Donna herself.

Jim noticed that the floor had been scrubbed. There was a pasty white layer of soap across its shiny surface.

He glanced over at Rob's roommate, Petrie, who lay with his face to the wall. Asleep or awake, he was ignoring Jim.

"You been having nightmares again, old buddy?" Jim walked over to him and crouched down. "Needing to clean up after yourself?"

Rob looked him in the eye.

This was unusual for a sociopath, to be cowering like this, afraid of a world that existed only as a delusion. Unless something had threatened Rob's sense of himself as being real. Unless he had, for the first time in his existence, been made to feel small by someone.

But what or who could've done that?

Rob whispered, "Now I know why. It wasn't the eyes, Mr. Anderson, it wasn't the eyes at all. She showed me."

He unclenched his hands, something in them.

Something all smeared and red.

Curled hairs at its fringe.

Skeins of flesh, a loose tapestry unraveled in his hands.

"Damn," Jim said, standing, staggering backward.

"It wasn't in her eyes, I thought it was, but it wasn't. It was in her purse," Rob said, holding the thing in his hands up, like a supplicant, for Jim's inspection. "Just like my mother's purse. It's in it. That's where her why was. She showed me. She SHOWED me."

CHAPTER 9

Three hours later, after docking the Westcoaster, Trey Campbell was dialing his work number from a pay phone on Catalina. Carly was just coming out of the rest room several yards away. She had slipped into navy blue shorts and a turquoise T-shirt, and was stopping every few feet to get her sandals on.

Trey waved to her so she'd see him. She looked up, wrinkling her nose. She would know the call was about work. They hadn't had a decent vacation in six years, between her finishing her master's and starting with the county, handling adoptions, and his obsessive work habits (and he hated work, but could not keep from being a workaholic, as lazy as he dreamed of being).

And then, that thing. That incident. Accident. With the gun. It was always there, in the back of his head. He couldn't sleep some nights thinking about it. When he finally could sleep, he often dreamed about it, as if it were happening all over again.

"This is Campbell. I need to talk to Jim Anderson, Building D," Trey said into the mouthpiece, and the call was transferred.

Carly didn't even come over. She went to get her sun block from the boat. He watched her. She looked like she belonged here, a beautiful woman in a beautiful town. The slant of light, flat and broad. The town beneath the sun, layered in the harshness of the day. He saw some children with their father walking past Carly on the dock. The children were all laughing. One held a large sea bass high in the air. Young couples in brightly colored clothes strolled along the promenade. An old man sat on a bench outside the drugstore, clutching a cane, watching all the tourists with a look of disgust on his face. Carly got her sun block and walked back up to the promenade, ducking into a souvenir shop. The colors of the small seafront town were all pastel blues and yellows and greens. It was like an old painting to him, a town from another time, a resort of perfection and sleepy eyes.

The *Catalina Express* was docking a little ways up, with yet more tourists ready to disembark. Trey had hoped that not too many people would be on the island yet since it was midweek. As it turned out, the place was packed. At least they had the boat. Later on, maybe he'd take Mark and Teresa out around one of the coves and let the baby-sitter have a break for a few hours. *That would be nice. Or maybe just lounge around at the rented cottage, read, watch television, relax.*

Finally, Jim's voice came on the line. "Billy. Glad you're around."

"I'm not really around. You beeped?"

"Had some trouble this morning. Just thought I'd report in. It's under control, but shook me up some."

Jim had that deadpan way of speaking, as if nothing were very important. But there was an edge to his voice.

"Someone bite his tongue off?" It was the joke at Darden, because between eye poppings and tongue bitings, there wasn't a lot else for the psych techs to joke about.

"A little worse," Jim said.

"Drop the other shoe." Trey sighed. He knew how bad things could get. He had seen men and women do things to themselves and each other which were, to him, like coming upon a vision of hell.

Some static on the phone line.

"Jim?" Trey said. "What was that? I didn't hear you."

Jim Anderson said, "I said, Robby-boy somehow got hold of a play toy. A real vagina. Only this one didn't have a woman attached."

CHAPTER 10

Christ. Trey Campbell held his breath for a few seconds. It was more a prayer than a curse. He brought the receiver down from his ear and inhaled the clean salt air. Closed his eyes. Tried to block out the image that was forming in his head. Then, back to the phone. "Fallon did that?"

"Other bad news. I think it's Donna Howe."

Trey remembered catching Rob Fallon flirting with Donna, and warning her about how Rob behaved. Trey felt tears coming to his eyes. *Poor Donna.* They hadn't had a murder on the premises in thirteen years. "I *know* it was Donna. Dammit."

A pause on the line.

Then Jim said, "We haven't found the body yet. Fallon isn't talking about why he did it or where he put the rest of her. Cops have been checking the lockers and the ceiling, but still no corpse. Since Fallon didn't run, the cops aren't putting us in lockdown, so at least it's not the hell we had when Kmetko ran in 'ninety-one. Fallon's having his usual field day, but even he's acting weird. Fallon claims Donna isn't dead. Had to give him some more meds . . ." Jim kept chattering nervously about Rob and poor Donna, but Trey barely heard him.

He was remembering something, something about genitals.

He interrupted Jim. "Jimmy, it's not Rob. That's not his M.O., you know that. Eyes and heads are his thing. Go check on Hatcher."

Another pause.

"Jim?"

"Billy," Jim said, "are you nuts? She's bound and gagged—"

"Look, it's her M.O. Body parts. Surgery. Rob might've killed Donna, but the genitals are consistent with Hatcher. Check on her now. Right this minute. I'll stay on the line."

Trey watched as Carly finally came out of the souvenir shop, her hands full of postcards. She walked toward him, her sunglasses slipping down her nose a little. As she got closer, he smelled the coconut oil. She smelled delicious. She managed a smile and held up a postcard of a mermaid. "I'm going to send this to Mitch, he'll love it, and Rick and Kathe, I got one for them too—wait, wait." She sorted through the cards.

She brought one out but must've noticed how distracted he was.

"What's up?"

He sighed, reached over, and put his arm around her. "A woman at work. Killed."

"Oh, my God," she gasped, and through clenched teeth said, "I hate your job. We did come here to think about you getting out of there with both eyes intact, right?"

He kissed her forehead, tasting coconut oil.

Jim came back on the line. "Billy?"

"She's not there, is she?"

"Billy—Rita says Hatcher's in her room. She's cuffed, still doped up from last night's meds, face cover still intact. . . ."

"Well, thank God for that. Hope Rob talks."

"Me too. If anything else happens, I'll beep."

"Okay. Thanks. And Tuesday, buddy," Trey said.

"Oh, yeah, Tuesday," Jim said.

Trey hung the phone up. Caught his breath. The fresh air was a relief. He realized that his breathing had been shallow ever since he thought of Agnes Hatcher. Sometimes he held his breath when he went into her room at Darden. Sometimes he held his breath when he heard her name. He inhaled deeply, shaking his head.

"What's all the stuff about Tuesday?" Carly asked.

"Well, besides being my first day back, he owes me fifty bucks. I told him something would screw up during my first vacation in years."

"He's an easy mark. Never bet against a sure thing."

Although he didn't completely believe it, Trey said, "Well, they can handle it on their end. They don't need me."

"Repeat after me: They don't need me, they don't need me, they can handle it," Carly said mock hypnotically. And then softly, "I'm so sorry about that woman."

"Me too." He shook his head. "She was having a fling with a patient. I saw it coming. I spoke with her about it. Next week I was going to take her out of that building and put her in another one. I probably should've fired her for getting involved, but I wasn't completely positive that anything was going on. I should've acted sooner. I didn't think she'd really fall for his act. She must've trusted him."

Carly's eyes widened. "You're kidding. Why would someone do something that stupid?"

"If you're at all vulnerable, and inexperienced, it happens. The guy's a sociopath. He found her weakness, and he went for it. She probably had never been in love before, and here's this young, good-looking guy who seems perfectly normal, and she's with him all night long, talking, laughing. Only she doesn't know that he's planning something for her. He's not like she is, he does things for effect, he does things only to get something for himself, because to him, she's not even real. To him she's just an object, like a lamp or a doll."

"Sometimes," Carly began, "when I hear about those things at your job, it makes me not so sure that we live in a decent world."

"Yeah, I know."

"I sure hope nothing else happens this week."

"He'll beep me if anything does," Trey said, holding the beeper up, about to put it back in his shirt pocket.

Carly made a grab for it, got the beeper, dropped her postcards, and said, "Oh, no, he won't. No more beeps." She laughed, and he wasn't sure what she was going to do. She took it, and ran down to the boat, and by the time she threw the beeper in the water, he was running for her.

"No, Carly!" he said, but as soon as the infernal thing fell beneath the slight waves, he was somehow relieved. He had never been far from that beeper for the past ten years. Then, to his own surprise, he started laughing. He knew it was awful to be laughing after a coworker had been murdered, probably sadistically. Nothing surprised or shocked him anymore, not after what he'd seen at Darden: the eyes smeared on the walls, the man who tore his own penis and testicles off with his bare hands, the woman who took a lightbulb, broke it, and in front of him and Jim, sliced off her nipples. It wasn't just a hospital for the criminally insane, and it was more than just the archaic notion of a madhouse, it was humanity laid bare, with both its brilliance and its brutality.

Trey stood at the edge of the dock on Catalina Island and laughed, shocked that he could do so after the morning's tragedy. He could not stop for ten minutes.

He had trained Donna Howe in procedure.

He had tried to reach out to Rob Fallon, to try to make him understand how he had hurt people and how that was bad.

He had failed on all counts.

He could not stop them from doing what they were compelled to do.

Donna Howe needed love, and Rob Fallon needed scalps.

It almost occurred to him then.

CHAPTER 11

They ate lunch at one of the restaurants along the boardwalk. Trey ordered yellowtail and a salad, but didn't eat very much of it. Carly carefully avoided seafood, and opted for a hamburger. Neither spoke much during lunch. Trey's mind was on Darden State again, and he was fighting to put it out of his head.

At one point she asked, "Are you going to be okay?"

He nodded.

"If you want to talk about this, we can," she said, and sipped her coffee.

After lunch they strolled back up to the small cottage they were renting, set up against the hills just beyond the Zane Grey Hotel. As far as Trey was concerned, the place was costing them a small fortune, but it was beautiful, had a washer, dryer, a swimming pool, and a deck with a barbecue. In the mornings he and Carly sat up in bed and watched deer cross the yard, heading for the stand of trees up against the hills. He joked that it seemed nicer than their house in Redlands. Once he saw the cottage, nestled as it was up in the hills above the sea, he knew it would be worth any expense. The sitter, too, was fairly expensive, but not much more so than Mrs. Quinlan, who watched the kids after school back home.

"And this is our summer vacation," Carly had reminded him. "What little there is of it."

Catalina's living area was small. The town of Avalon was no more than several streets that ended almost abruptly beyond these first hills. It reminded him of postcards he'd seen of the Mediterranean—blue and white and yellow buildings on a hillside over a blue expanse of sea. The town was packed in tight with shops and summer houses, as if these were exiled from the rest of the island. There were campgrounds and nature preserves beyond Avalon, but most of the tourists stayed in town and rode the golf carts around the hills for entertainment, or took horses up the trails, or the glass-bottomed boat out into the harbor. He and Carly had come to the island years before and stayed a few weekends, and then had forgotten its existence as a quick Southern California getaway until they planned this trip. The choice had been either spend the cash and drive up the coast to do a little touring, or drop a bundle on a little seaside place. Carly had won, as usual, because she wanted something relaxing, away from cars and especially from work.

Now, with the beeper buried at sea, she got everything she wanted.

The screen door to the cottage was closed, but the inner door was wide open. Trey didn't like this. Although Catalina seemed a safe enough place, he wasn't sure that it was far enough from the criminals and gangsters of the mainland. He opened the screen door and went in ahead of his wife. Something about that morning's call to Jimmy Anderson made him nervous. Okay, so the Hatcher woman was still in her cuffs, still in bed . . . but the genitals in Fallon's hand just didn't add up for Fallon. Fallon would kill you as look at you, but he wasn't a sadist, and his problems didn't seem to center around sexuality.

Carly said, "What is it? Something wrong?"

"Just my instinct," Trey said, turning around to look at the silhouette of his wife against the sun's reflection on the Pacific. "You want a beer?"

"I want you, big boy," she said, stepping into the house, letting the door slam behind her. "Actually, what I really want is to get back to my big fat murder mystery. I wonder when Jenny'll be back with the kids."

Then they both heard a loud splash out back in the pool, and Trey went to get a beer from the fridge. "I guess Jenny's back. And I guess Mark's still trying to swim."

"Get me an iced tea and meet me out poolside, stud," Carly said. "And bring the camera—I don't want to miss Marky's first swim."

Jenny Reed, the local girl they'd hired for the week, was trying to teach Mark how to do the Australian crawl, but the six-year-old would have none of it. Teresa, eleven, was an expert swimmer and had never been afraid of the water. She sat on the edge of the small kidney-shaped pool and sneered at her brother's chicken-heartedness. They both seemed to have wisdom beyond their years to Trey, who often felt that his children were smarter than their old man.

Carly had a book in one hand and was pointing at Mark with the other. "Just pretend you're like *Free Willy,*

Mark, you know, diving over the rocks.'' Then she set the book on her lap and started reading, looking up only now and then to give Trey camera instructions.

Ever since they'd bought the video camera, when Mark had been a newborn, Trey had hated lugging it all over the place, but he had to admit that the memories it preserved were worth it. He got a nice shot of Carly shooing him away so she could read. And then Teresa, making a neat dive from the edge of the pool. Mark just sat, his feet in the water, and refused to get in. When he turned the camera to Jenny, she blushed. She was sixteen and blond, and had a kind of sparkling personality. She didn't talk a lot, but she seemed smart, and the kids loved her.

Trey turned the video camera back to Mark, who looked at the water, now less afraid for some reason.

Mark told the camera, ''I can see me in the pool.''

Trey laughed. ''You can? Why don't you tell us what *me* looks like.''

''Me doesn't look scared, I know that.''

Teresa asked, ''Oh, so you're not a 'fraidy-cat anymore?''

In the camera, with the sunlight filtering through the bougainvillea-shrouded trellis work, Trey's daughter looked as if she were only half there—the other half in shade, vanishing. She looked so much like her mother, it was amazing. She would be just as beautiful, and she was smarter than her old man.

Back to Mark, who said, ''I guess me isn't a 'fraidy-cat. Look,'' he said, touching his reflection. ''Me is gone.''

And then he stood on the edge of the pool, looked at his father and the camera, and said, ''Is it okay, Daddy, to get in?''

"Of course, Marky. Just jump. The water's not deep. Jenny'll help if you have trouble."

"I don't want her to," his son said. "Will you help, Daddy, if something bad happens? Like if I can't get out? Like if something's down at the bottom?"

"Nothing to be afraid of."

His son shook his head. "Lots of things down at the bottom."

"It's just like the mirror at home, son. That's all."

Mark looked at the pool, at his father, into the video camera's eye. Just as he was about to jump in, Trey had an urge to stop him, grab him, and keep him from getting in, to keep him from anything that might hurt him.

Keep him safe.

But a second later, Mark was splashing around the pool, doing a modified dog paddle.

Carly looked up from her book, took her sunglasses off, and cheered.

Trey kept shooting the video, because he knew it would be archival. One day when Mark was twenty-five and a father himself, Trey could show this to him, show him how scary it could be to watch your son take a step toward the unknown.

It wasn't until one-thirty in the afternoon that his brain had pieced together what had happened back at Darden State that morning.

And what it might mean to him if his hunch was correct.

Jenny took the kids down to go to the movies. Carly was taking a nap. He heard sea gulls overhead, crying out.

Trey made some coffee and picked up the phone.

He dialed work. What he had thought of earlier in the day had grown into a theory.

Donna Howe needed love, and Rob Fallon needed scalps.

The phone rang six or seven times. He knew that when there was an attack or disappearance on the ward, there was so much confusion that the phones were not always attended to. He had once been there during a riot, and he and his staff were so busy that they hadn't even bothered to buzz in the riot control police, who would've ended the problem swiftly.

Run for the phone, Jim. Come on.

He felt certain of the outcome of the call before the line was even picked up on the other end.

CHAPTER 12

Trey said, "Jim? I want you to go check Agnes Hatcher's bed."

"I told you already, we checked it. Look, Fallon's in the bouncing room, and we've had the cops come through looking for the body—"

Trey cut him off. "I don't give a damn, Jimmy, now just do what I tell you. Anybody feed her yet? Hatcher have lunch?"

An almost petulant silence ensued. Then, "I don't know."

Trey sighed, exasperated. He took a couple of deep breaths, because his first instinct was to chew Jim Anderson out. But Anderson was good. He generally knew what he was doing. He just didn't know Agnes Hatcher all that well. "I'm willing to bet no one has fed her. I'm willing to bet she's lying in that bed with her restraints loose, waiting for someone to come feed her."

"Here, Billy, I've got the log." Trey could hear the

papers being riffled through. He could almost hear the desperation in Jim's voice, as if Jim were beginning to fear that Trey's hunch might be correct. "It says—all right, it says she hasn't eaten yet. Says she was still knocked out at breakfast. Asleep. Her meds were heavy last night. She didn't fall asleep until four-thirty A.M. Paulsen did the lunch log—she told me that she went into Hatcher's room today at one with the bedpan, only she was still asleep." Jim paused. He whispered into the phone, "Billy, they heard her snoring for God's sakes." Another pause.

Trey was sure Jim was getting worried. It was like they all had a panic button related to some of the inmates. A panic button that was so easy to push, and when pushed, a bomb went off somewhere.

In a more normal tone Jim continued. "You know what a live wire Hatcher can be. Paulsen decided not to wake her. I know it's negligent, but you know nobody likes dealing with Hatcher. They'll try feeding her in about twenty minutes."

Trey cursed under his breath. "No, Jim, here's what you're going to do. Get a couple of the big guys—maybe Howie and Dave—and get down to Hatcher's room right now, and if a cop's around, get him too. My take is that Hatcher is lying there in that bed with blood on her face, and her hands are loose. She's tried this before. This is what she did on the outside."

Jim gasped. It occurred to Trey that Jim was not aware of the method of Hatcher's crimes.

"Look, Jim. Before D ward nicknamed her the Gorgon, she was called the Surgeon. She operated on people while they were still alive. She removed parts of their bodies based on what she felt was wrong with them. If Rob Fallon was having sex with Donna Howe, Agnes Hatcher would see her sex organs as what was wrong with Donna. What was causing her to be bad. I'm telling you, it's Hatcher's M.O." Trey waited for a response, but all he heard was Jim's breathing. "I'm telling you, she's lying in that bed waiting for someone to pull the covers back. She's waiting to attack again. When you go in, be ready for a fight. Get some more restraints. Take a metal rod with you, something you can pry between her teeth if she tries to bite and lock her jaws on you." It took so long for Jim to respond again, Trey felt like slamming the phone down.

"She's drugged up," Jim said. "You'd think she was a pit bull. She's just a patient. She's got so much junk in her, I doubt she can lift a finger."

Trey chuckled at the younger man's naïveté. Graveyard humor was a staple of Ward D. "You've seen her for only the past four years, Jimmy. I knew her when. I know what she can do."

"Okay, boss, I'll do what you want. And if you're wrong, you owe me a hundred come Tuesday, deal?"

"Deal. Look, my beeper's not working. Just call me back," Trey said. He gave Jim the number to the cottage, and then hung up.

CHAPTER 13

In his office at Darden State, Jim Anderson scratched his head. The entire morning had been like a migraine about to descend upon him, and he had swallowed enough aspirin to kill a horse. Still, his head was pounding. The flickering overhead lights, all fluorescent bulbs needing replacement, compounded the headache.

It made him angry that he had to follow Campbell's orders again, given all the crap coming down that morning. He'd been hoping to prove himself to his superior. It seemed now that he was proving just how incompetent he could be at handling problems. He glanced at Rita Paulsen, who was pushing a rolling tray of meds and juice cups. Two psych techs were walking with the pretty recreational therapist down the hall toward the game room. A patient was screaming in the south wing, but that was for Lewis to handle.

Who would've thought that somewhere on this hall

a woman was murdered, her body hidden, her genitals cut off?

The police were still there, an invisible presence, for they were down in Ward A getting coffee. Jim didn't feel they were that necessary, except for incarcerating Rob Fallon yet again, this time in a less psychiatric-friendly prison—but that would come later, after Rob had undergone yet another trial for murder and another psychiatric evaluation. Cops just got in the way, Jim thought. They tended to be brutish and nasty about the inmates; Jim felt a kind of paternal concern for the psychos on his shift. *Thank God they're out of my hair for now.*

But they'd be back soon, sniffing around for Donna's body. Jim had no doubt that she was stuffed into some locker or cupboard somewhere in the hall. It wasn't the first time a staff member had bitten it, but it was the first time to Jim's knowledge that it had been a woman murdered. And one as seemingly competent as Donna Howe. Only Rob Fallon would know where her body lay, and he wasn't going to start talking till his shrink showed up.

"Rita," Jim said. "You want to hear something funny?"

Rita Paulsen looked up from the tray. She was not very bright, nor was she particularly competent, but she was tough on the job. She had a face like an angel, but she could hold down a patient in the middle of a psychotic rage if the situation arose. She was definitely an asset to the ward. "What's up?" she asked.

"That was Campbell on the phone. He thinks that Hatcher killed Donna. Says she's in her bed waiting for us." He laughed thinking of how absurd the idea was. He had a laugh like a bull elephant. It echoed down the ward. "Ever since he shot that guy in his backyard, he's been completely paranoid."

Rita shook her head. "Can't blame him, given this place. But let's face it, if Hatcher had wanted to get us, she would've done it earlier. I was in there. She was snoring like a baby, you know, same old same old." Rita looked at her watch. "Well, we can test out his theory. You want to come with me to go feed the Gorgon?"

Because Hatcher seemed smarter and more watchful than the other patients, everyone was afraid of her eyes. Although that was not the reason for the cloth over her face. The cloth was there because if the staff needed to feed her or be anywhere near her face, she had a mean overbite. Still, the face cloth added to the myth of the Gorgon.

"Okay," Jim said. "Sure. Let's go feed the Gorgon. But I don't want to look at her. Last time I did, it was like she was studying me for something."

"For her next meal." Rita Paulsen grinned. "Ready?"

CHAPTER 14

Agnes Hatcher's room had been an enormous walk-in refrigerator twenty years before. Then it was converted into a room for a patient named Emily Freund, who had murdered her children and spent most of her life trying to tear the flesh off her own bones. The refrigerator walls were knocked out, and the room expanded, but it was again reinforced with steel doors. Most patients were able to come and go at certain times of the day, but Agnes, owing to her constant violent and aggressive tendencies, was restrained almost round the clock. In the afternoon she was allowed to stand for four hours, restrained with her arms up in straps and her feet secured near the floor. She had one hour of exercise a day, in another room, almost a cell, by herself. A television monitor played an exercise tape, if she so chose to do calisthenics. But the majority of the rest of her life would be spent in that bed, strapped in, face covered. To outsiders this often seemed horrifying.

But then, as the therapists, doctors, and psych techs and orderlies knew, this was Agnes Hatcher.

This was the Gorgon.

She had been a patient at Darden after being transferred from another hospital up the coast because she had caused a riot among the patients. A very liberal-thinking doctor had given her a certain amount of freedom, believing that her psychosis arose from a childhood of abuse and deprivation. She rewarded her doctor by operating on him as he was held down by the weight of concrete blocks, without the benefit of anesthesia. They said he lived for six more hours, but when he was found, he was begging for death—which came within minutes of the paramedics' arrival.

At Darden she had bitten off three fingers of an orderly within two hours of her check-in. Within twenty-four hours she was under constant restraint.

Outside Darden's walls she had surgically removed a woman's liver on her coffee table, and played with it for a while. She claimed that the woman was a recovering alcoholic who had lapsed one too many times. Her liver had been her problem. She had murdered a police officer, which was the crime that led to her arrest and the discovery of all her other murders. When the police arrested her, it took six men, and she had to be beaten into submission. On the walls of her house they found dozens of notes with the addresses of the policemen who had ever bothered her, and their children's schools; also, of doctors who had examined her, and their families, and of lawyers who had been unkind or threatening to her over bad debts. Others too—names and addresses to which she had no apparent connection—were slated for torture and death. On some of them she intended to perform her perverse surgery.

She had been planning on slicing off parts of their bodies as souvenirs.

In her home they found a collection of penises, bladders, livers, hearts, and lungs, and one jar of preserved brains. Some had come from animals, some from unidentified humans. She owned several surgical instruments, most of which had been stolen from hospitals over the years. She had created her own, using hybrids of fingernail scissors and metal nail files and other household items. She had turned the small den of her home in Pasadena into her surgery, and there was enough evidence of carnage there that one of the investigating officers had remarked, "Forensics is going to spend years trying to figure out what belongs to who."

She had been a high school teacher in Pasadena for several years.

She believed strongly in reincarnation, and that life was a continuum from one incarnation to the next; she attended All Saints Church, and considered herself a heretical Episcopalian.

She had graduated Phi Beta Kappa from the University of California at Berkeley. With a degree in forensic science.

At the time of her arrest she was a teacher and lecturer at various police academies in the Southern California area.

She was a member of the Junior League.

Her ancestors had come over on the *Mayflower*. She was a member of the Daughters of the American Revolution, but had not been to a meeting in several years.

She contributed heavily to the Children's Defense Fund and the World Wildlife Fund.

She voted Republican whenever she voted, but leaned toward a libertarian philosophy.

She was a member in good standing of Mensa.

A neighbor, just before Agnes's arrest, had been trying to set her up with his cousin.

She had subscription tickets to the L.A. Philharmonic.

She was the Gorgon.

Rita opened the door to Agnes Hatcher's room and flicked the light up. "Time to wake up, Miss Hatcher."

CHAPTER 15

In the bed, the patient moaned.

Waking up.

"Jesus," Jim Anderson said, stepping around Rita Paulsen, "has she been spitting up blood?"

A spackling of red was on the olive-drab blanket.

In his mind he knew that Campbell had been right. The Gorgon must've killed Donna Howe. She must've somehow gotten loose. She was playing a game with them. He held his breath for a second, wondering if he should call Howie and Dave into the room to help hold Hatcher down.

But he saw her hand; it was in the restraint. It was definitely in the restraint.

The cloth face cover was soaked red.

"It wasn't like that earlier," Rita said, sounding a bit defensive as well as confused.

Jim knew that Rita was occasionally negligent. He

knew, considering all the black marks in her file, that she might be fired for not noticing something like this on her rounds. Maybe, he thought, with the lights out, maybe you wouldn't see the red. Maybe you wouldn't even look at where Hatcher's face was, because you thought of her as the Gorgon and didn't even like thinking of her as a human being.

His first impulse was to remove the face cover, but he remembered for a second what Campbell had told him.

Or warned him about.

No cops in the hall, and no metal rods on hand. He looked at Rita. "You ready to see her?"

Rita Paulsen shuddered a little. "Whenever."

"She may attack. Stand back a little, okay?"

Rita moved to the side, but did not seem very nervous.

At least not as nervous as Jim Anderson felt inside. He figured if he pulled the face cover off swiftly, then maybe he could jump back. It was important not to lean into inmates like this. It was important to be ready to step backward, so that if they lunged, you'd be safe.

Cautiously, he went over to the edge of the bed.

The hand in the restraint, what he could see of it, twitched slightly, then dropped as if Hatcher were asleep and dreaming.

Jim checked his own balance to ensure that if she did make a grab for him, he could move back without falling.

He leaned over the inmate and lifted the face cover.

Beneath it, a mass of blood.

A woman's eyes staring up at him, as if she were trying to scream but could not with her mouth, nor would her vocal cords muster much more than a reedy whine.

Only with her eyes, wide open, could she signal pain and suffering.

He knew those eyes.

His first thought was: *Campbell was wrong.*

CHAPTER 16

Trey Campbell had grown experienced at blocking bad memories. This was one of the side effects of working at Darden. For those psych techs and orderlies who could not block out or deny the work environment reality, there were often breakdowns or burnouts. Several psychiatrists over the past three decades had left Darden, never to practice their craft again because they no longer believed in the gods of Jung and Freud. Occasionally, there were suicide attempts.

But Trey could not block the memory that hit him full force as he sat back after hanging up the phone with Anderson.

Trey was twenty-two, a new hire at Darden. He was going for walks with Hatcher in the garden. He believed that Agnes Hatcher was somewhere inside the abused woman beside him. He believed her childhood had been taken away and her brain had been damaged through torture. She was smart, he thought. He believed then that if a person was smart enough, she could be rehabilitated in some form. He played chess with her often; he brought her books, mainly Charles Dickens novels, which she loved.

And then, one day, he slipped.

He told her something he regretted as soon as the words were out of his mouth. "It's Balantine. He has this theory about human behavior."

Agnes bent down to pick a flower. "Look at these roses," she said, glancing back at him. Her blond hair fell to one side of her neck. She was pretty, although the faintest scar tissue could still be seen just at the corners of her eyes, and along her neck. "The psychiatrist? I like him."

"I just don't think you need to be in those restraints all the time. That's all. You've proven to me that your illness is chemical and behavioral. Balantine talks about my patients like they're—" He searched for the appropriate word.

"Monsters?" she asked. She stood up again. "You believe in me, don't you?"

"I believe that no human being should be shut away and hog-tied." That was when he knew he had said too much. She had a way about her though. Something that inspired confidence. An almost hypnotic quality. For a moment he felt like the patient, and she, the psych tech. "Let's go back. You're due for some meds."

"I don't like Balantine," she said. He watched her face for signs of tension, but she seemed perfectly balanced, perfectly relaxed.

It wasn't until he came upon her two weeks later that he knew he had made a mistake of gargantuan proportion.

She had just gone into her room from one of her walks. The psychiatrist, Balantine, had been there with his clipboard and drawings for her to examine. Agnes was already on every pill known to the medical community at that time. Every pill that would subdue the strongest man.

Trey could not forget: walking down the hallway, smiling at one of the nurses, who smiled back. The way his head was throbbing from a midafternoon headache. The smell of the laundry, for back then, it had been on his ward. That clean soap smell that seemed to cover all the other smells of Darden State. He was thinking of the fishing trip he and his buddies were going to take in a few days—deep-sea fishing off San Pedro, three hours out. He had thrown in his sixty bucks toward the boat rental. He was broke for the week from that, but he would catch enough fish to fill his freezer and then some.

He walked past Agnes Hatcher's room, glancing through the thick glass windows. Sometimes he nodded to her as he went.

He stopped, turned, and went back to her door.

Through the window he saw Agnes leaning over the psychiatrist like a lioness over her prey.

She turned and saw him.

A faint oval of red around her mouth.

The psychiatrist's skin had been peeled back along his scalp.

She had been trying to open his skull up to find his brain. After hours of operations and grafts, Balantine survived, but never practiced at Darden again.

Later, restrained, she told Trey, "He lived in his head. I wanted to set him free."

It was the last time Trey Campbell had ever seen Agnes Hatcher without her face cover on.

It was the beginning of her obsession with him. An obsession that would last right up to the present summer day, July second, when he was thirty-six.

Trey took three aspirin and swallowed them dry. He stood in the kitchen of the rented house and kept trying to block those old memories. *We're safe,* he told himself. *We're in a cottage on an island twenty-six miles off the coast, about one hundred and forty miles from Darden State. She's in her restraints. She can't do anything to us. To me.*

Carly sauntered into the kitchen and said, "How about a little romance to take your mind off this?"

CHAPTER 17

"Now? I thought you were going to take a nap," Trey said, wiping his hands clean with a washcloth. He hadn't heard back from Jim Anderson just yet. He had gone to make some fresh orange juice, but spilled juice all over the counter instead. Carly stood in the doorway in his blue T-shirt that barely covered her thighs.

"Yes, now," she said. "I couldn't sleep. We have the place to ourselves for a few hours . . . why not now?"

Trey got a sponge and wiped the rest of the counter and cutting board clean of juice. He dropped the sponge in the sink.

His mind was still on Agnes Hatcher. He found that the more he tried to block his fear about her from his mind, the more she seemed to be engraved in his thoughts. He glanced at Carly. Strange to think of both Carly and the Gorgon, as if one face was, briefly, superimposed over the other. Agnes Hatcher was not a bad-looking woman either; different, though, petite, blond, an elfish kind of face. Almost innocent. And then those eyes . . . When Agnes Hatcher flashed them at you, it was like a lightning bolt, it was like twin lasers cutting through your skin. She was only a human being, but Trey Campbell had seen those small blue eyes enough to know they contained the ferocity of a tiger.

Carly frowned. It must've been obvious to her that his mind was elsewhere.

"Trey, just you and me and Catalina." Carly walked right up to him and threw her arms around his waist. "The smell of the ocean, the clean air, the breeze . . . what are we waiting for, violins and roses? When we get back, it'll be nothing but work for months to come. No getaways, no times to ourselves. Just enough time for kids and jobs. But right now . . ." She brought a hand up to his collar and stroked the edge of his chin. She let her hand slide down to his chest. "Sometimes I forget how to even be romantic—where to put my arms, how to relax, how to be just like when we met, when it was you and me and chemistry. Remember?"

Trey nodded, grinning. "All that stuff at work," he said. "It's just got me so wound up." He felt incredibly warm with her, comfortable, as if they were not two people, but one person, complete, together. They'd had the roughest year of their marriage—not because they didn't love each other or care for each other, but because the kids and the job and school all seemed to conspire to keep them unconnected.

And that dark morning with the shadow and the white flash from gunshot. The memory always threatened the horizon for him, like a coming storm. He shut his eyes, opened them, as if it would stop the memory from coming.

She rested her head against his chest. "No work talk."

"Jim's supposed to call back soon."

"Fine. Then he'll call back soon and you can deal

with it. But if we have even a half hour to ourselves in this love nest, I say let's take advantage of it.'' She looked up at him; he could tell that she was trying to see if interest was stirring. She kissed him rather aggressively.

Her lips tasted like the sea. He closed his eyes. Her taste was always wonderful, sweet and sour at the same time. He brought his arms around her, his hands exploring her back down to her thighs. The sensations he felt were both exciting and soothing.

She wiped her lips across his face, to his chin, his neck. He kissed the rim of her ear. As if by instinct, he lifted her up, his hands beneath her, her legs wrapping around him, and carried her over to the couch. The blinds were up, but there was nothing in view other than the pool and the hills. A hawk circled above the hills against a blue and white sky.

She whispered, ''I love you, I love you.''

He, too, whispered the warmest things he knew, and felt burning and strong as he made love to his wife, the woman he had dreamed of loving since the moment he'd first seen her. She moved beneath him, and his body responded. In the last moment he glanced out the porch doors, out to the hawk in the sky, and watched it dive after some unseen prey, dive down until it was invisible among the trees.

CHAPTER 18

Jim Anderson, leaning over Agnes Hatcher's bed at Darden State Hospital, felt his heart freeze.

For a moment he could not move.

For a moment time stopped.

Campbell was wrong, he thought.

Hatcher's not about to attack anyone.

He knew the face of the woman in the bed.

He knew the woman.

Not Hatcher.

Not the Gorgon.

Jim Anderson felt nothing but stark terror when he saw the woman.

CHAPTER 19

Beneath the face cover, beneath the blankets:
Donna Howe.
She was still alive.

PART TWO

CHAPTER 20

It was still light out on Catalina Island when Trey Campbell awoke. He checked the clock: not even four yet. Night would not come for another four hours or so. He would not sleep tonight, he knew. He would need to have a drink or two to stop the whirlwind in his head—thinking about Hatcher and what he had done once by letting her be free. Thinking about death, and the man he had shot in a dark morning. All swirling around his job, which was the most insane job anyone could have.

And yet he had felt he had contributed some good to the system. He had to believe that.

During his nap he'd been having a dream, not about Agnes Hatcher or Carly, but about his mother and father and brother. And about the first time he knew about people. The first time he *really* knew. He was six, and his father and mother were taking him and his brother to New York to go sight-seeing. They walked along Sixth

Avenue at dusk, and he had lost sight of them. He didn't know where his mother was. His father had already gone off to some business dinner, but his mother and brother were supposed to be there. He looked at the people all walking, rushing, running, stomping, but he could not see his mother. Finally, he went up to a doorman who he thought was a policeman because of his uniform, and asked if he knew where his mother was.

The doorman looked at him, and the six-year-old Trey Campbell knew then that the doorman was insane, and would've been willing to do something awful to a little boy like Trey, except for the fact that Trey's mother, right at that moment, came up and grabbed him by the hand and hurried off down the avenue, scolding him for not keeping up. Trey looked back at the doorman, who was still watching him. It had been Trey's first run-in with what they called on B Ward a DM, which stood for Dangerous Motherfucker. All the psych techs knew them on sight, sometimes on smell, and Trey had developed his sense for them early in life. Trey sometimes wondered about the people whose lives were touched and ended by that doorman in New York.

Trey Campbell, thirty-six, leaned back on the couch. Carly was asleep in the crevice of his arm and chest. She snored lightly. He was naked; she had managed to retain the blue T-shirt through their lovemaking. The house was dark; the sky outside, pink. He wondered, for a second, about the kids, as he always did when he didn't know their whereabouts. But Jenny had taken them to the movie down at Monte Casino. Probably for ice cream cones and a walk afterward. Catalina was possibly the safest place to be in Southern California. What was he worried about?

After a few minutes he slid clumsily out from under Carly—she snarfled before settling down again on the couch. He stretched, yawned, and walked outside to the swimming pool.

He stood at the edge, looking at his shadowy reflection. There was the "me" that Marky had been talking about, the self that looked brave and strong, the reflection; but the flesh itself, to Trey, felt weak and tired and ready to throw in the towel. *Another week of vacation,* he thought, *that's all I need.*

He dove into the pool carefully, his hands in front of his head even beneath the water to protect himself in case the pool proved too shallow. But it was fine and deep, as small as it was. He came up gasping clean pure air.

It felt good to swim naked. He splashed around, feeling a bit like a kid again. Carly came out with some iced tea, and kept her T-shirt on no matter how much he begged.

"Well," she said after he'd gotten out of the water and was sitting buck naked on the pool recliner, "I guess you're feeling a little more frisky."

"A bit," he laughed, shaking his head in her direction to try to get her wet. "I guess I am not absolutely essential to the running of Darden State."

"Maybe not. But you're essential for the running of this family."

"Isn't it funny."

"What?"

"Oh, Carl, that we fight and get tense a lot at home, and then we come here and we're like two lovebirds on Spanish fly."

"My, my, Mr. Campbell, but you do flatter. And you know I hate being called Carl."

"Carly my baby"—he puckered his lips in a mock kiss—"*Carlotta Maria, la señorita más bonita en todo el mundo.*"

"You better keep worshipping me if you want to stay happy, bubba." Carly lay back and pointed to the sky. "Look at that sky. Pink and blue and yellow. Yikes, it's like a Spielberg movie."

Trey watched the play of pink and gold light out to the other side of the western hills of Catalina. The heat of the day had abated, and the feeling was bucolic. "Like a movie," he whispered, feeling drunk although he was not. "You and me live happily ever after, Carly, and nobody needs to call me again because the whole complex of Darden State's running smooth."

He reached across to where she sat, took her hand in his, squeezed it.

She gave him a strange look.

"I've got to tell you something," she said.

He raised his eyebrows, expecting some further protestation of love or lust.

"Something you might not be too happy about."

"Okay. Shoot."

"I unplugged the phone before. Now, honey, you were just starting to relax. I wasn't about to have that Jim person calling every ten minutes with some screwup that was going to keep us from enjoying ourselves. It's a hospital for the criminally insane, horrible things happen there. We don't need to bring them everywhere we go." And then, her head down, she said, "I'm sorry."

He felt himself tense up at first; but then he shook his head. "No biggie. You're right. I may be resigning soon anyway, right? Who needs 'em?"

But after a few minutes pretending to enjoy the view, he stood and excused himself to go take a shower.

On the way to the bathroom he plugged the bedroom phone back into its wall jack.

The phone rang immediately.

He picked it up. "Jim?"

The person on the other end of the line said nothing.
But he heard the breathing.
Her breathing.
The line went dead.

CHAPTER

21

"What's going on?" Carly asked. She stood in the doorway.

Trey Campbell sat on the bed, staring at the phone.

"Trey?"

He looked up at her. "She's out," he said.

"Who?"

His mouth was dry. "The Gorgon."

CHAPTER 22

Agnes Hatcher stared at the phone.

She wanted to say something, but she was afraid of being overheard. Someone had just walked back into the room. She couldn't trust the animals. She had spent most of the day squeezed into a crawl space above the acoustic tile on D Ward. The rest of the time, she'd hidden in a room.

Someone stood over her as she sat and thrummed her fingers on the desk's surface. One of the two who had come into the room, a man, was leaving. A man in a police uniform.

The woman who remained said, "I wish those cops would get out of our hair."

Agnes said nothing. Then she looked up at the woman who had just spoken and said, "Thanks for letting me use your phone."

"No problem." The woman was preoccupied, scanning a chart on a clipboard. The woman had fine features, but her forehead was wrinkled from stress. Her badge read *Kuehl.* Agnes had never seen her before. But then, Agnes had seen so few of their faces; likewise, few working on the ward had ever seen hers. The cloth cover was usually on her face, except when the animals fed her. Only then did she see a face or two. Only then could she begin to understand how these animals operated.

The waiting room was large and square. It contained three small desks, six chairs, and two potted plants. There was a television set suspended from the ceiling in the northeast corner. An *I Love Lucy* rerun was showing. Beneath the television set, a long window. Outside, the dried, matted lawn of Darden State, and two other buildings. Double doors led out to the sidewalk between the buildings. Agnes didn't know the layout of the other wards. She surmised that there was a diamond pattern to them, for each one had a courtyard. Beyond these buildings were the high fences, and beyond these, the canyon, and *freedom.*

Agnes Hatcher wore a dress that was loose and long for her frame. It was not the sort of fabric she would've chosen—these were Donna Howe's day clothes. Agnes had had to double-tuck the waist into the belt to keep from looking too clownish in the larger woman's clothes. The dress stank of barnyards, but Agnes tolerated it. She knew that a false move would land her back in the bed, back in the restraints. She'd had forty minutes after dealing with Donna Howe. She had washed in the sink in her room. She had shampooed her hair carelessly with yellow soap, and knew that it still contained some blood, matted at the nape of her neck. She had combed it out with her fingers before leaving her room. Donna's streetclothes had been in her locker, which was down the hall from her room. Because she knew that destiny was on her side, she was able to walk down the corridor undetected. She changed in the hall bathroom, and then tried to go outside, but had seen the police arrive. She went to sit in an elderly patient's room, opened a Bible, and began reading sections of it to the old man in the bed. When the police had come in to search the room, she had smiled at them and said, "Brothers, these poor souls, how desolate are their spirits." It was enough to make them leave her alone.

She watched the woman named Kuehl.

"Is something bad happening?" Agnes asked.

The woman didn't look up from her clipboard for a second. Then she said, "Oh, just some trouble with the patients."

"But that policeman who was just here? Did he know anything?"

"Nothing new." This time the woman named Kuehl looked at her. "You said your friend is meeting you?"

Agnes nodded. "My boyfriend. Jack. He's a doctor here. We're supposed to have a very late lunch. Is it four yet?"

The woman named Kuehl glanced at her wristwatch.

Agnes stood up from the desk. She walked over to the woman as the woman looked up from her watch.

"It's just past."

"Well," Agnes sighed, "then it's too late."

The woman looked at her face strangely, and Agnes worried for a second. She normally was never worried, but the woman seemed to notice something around Agnes's eyes.

"I think you're bleeding," the woman named Kuehl said.

"Oh, that. It's an old wound. I think I'll just leave a note for my friend," she said. "Do you have a pen?"

The woman reached into her breast pocket and withdrew the weapon, the cutter, the slicer, the skinner, the Bic ball-point pen.

CHAPTER 23

As Agnes Hatcher performed the surgery on the woman named Kuehl, it came back to her like a scent from the past, a day from her childhood remembered in a few seconds:

Her father would go into her room and find her makeup every morning and then throw it out or hide it so she couldn't find it. She was eleven, and her father was a puritan from the old school who didn't believe that girls her age wore any makeup unless they were practicing to become whores. So every day on her way to school she would walk up Laconia Boulevard, past the liquor store and the coffee shop, until she came to the Mobil station. She'd put coins in the machine to get a Coke, take a sip, and then ask the manager for the key to the rest room. She'd get it, unlock the room, and go in. It often smelled bad there, so she'd open her small purse and draw out a bottle of her mother's best perfume, usually Shalimar, which she had stolen from the dresser in her parents' bedroom. She'd spray some of it around the rest room, and apply a bit to the back of her neck. Then she'd take lipstick from her purse, and mascara, and a small compact with powder. These she would've bought at the drugstore and kept well concealed in a small music box in her room. Her father never opened the music box because it had once belonged to Agnes's grandmother. Her father hated her grandmother so much that he had smiled when he had heard the news of the old woman's death two years before.

Agnes considered this her magic hour, when she would transform herself at the Mobil rest room. From plain Agnes Hatcher to Francine, a young French goddess with dark eyelashes and rosy cheeks and cherry-red lips, a woman of intrigue and seductive charm. Francine had shapelier calves than Agnes, and she had a great deal of poise and joie de vivre. She would brush her hair out again so that it sparkled, and spray it carefully so as to keep it looking full and fresh all day long. Then she would finish her morning Coke, repack her supplies, pick her books up, and open the door to the rest room. School was two blocks farther. If she walked slowly she would not sweat too much, and so the boys in homeroom would look at her a certain way, which made her happy. She had found that if she lifted her dress just a bit as she sat down, they would smile at the glimpse of panties.

Then, after school, she would walk back to the Mobil station, go into the rest room, and wipe the makeup off with a Kleenex and some cold cream. She would wash her face and become, in her mind, plain Agnes again. Francine was there, still, in the mirror, left behind as Agnes trudged slowly home to a family that never fought or disagreed or said anything bad to one another.

It was on a Tuesday that this changed. Agnes walked up Laconia Boulevard by herself, but noticed someone watching her. She had just passed the liquor store, and looked at some of the champagnes advertised in the front window—she tried to see the reflection of the man who watched her in the glass, but all she saw was her own reflection and the sun's flat light. She turned to look at the man, shielding her eyes from the sunlight, thinking it was someone she knew. It was a man wearing chinos and boots, with a yellow shirt. It looked like a cowboy shirt, because there were lassos and horses embroidered on it. The man had blond hair and looked cute to her, even though she knew he must be nearly twice her age. She realized that he wasn't watching her at all. Apparently, he was just watching the road. His thumb was out and he had a green canvas duffel bag at his feet. He was hitchhiking.

She continued on to the Mobil station and waved to the two old men who sat out front. She tried to get a key to the rest room, but the attendant was busy, and the manager was nowhere to be seen. The manager was usually nice to her, and sometimes gave her a free Coke and patted her head. She missed him today; he was nicer than her father. Agnes bought a Coke and waited out by the garage bays, hoping to see the manager.

Then she went to try the rest room door.

Someone was inside the rest room and seemed to be taking forever. She waited almost ten minutes, and realized that she'd be late for school if she waited much longer. The transom to the women's room was open, and she heard the fan from within, and the sound of water running. And still the woman inside didn't come out.

Agnes knocked on the door. She was already finished with her Coke. Her books felt heavy in her arms.

The door to the men's room was open just a crack. The transom up top was open too, and there was no fan on, no sound at all. Agnes had never been in a men's rest room before, and had, frankly, been curious.

The men's room was shadowy. She pushed the door a bit farther open, and it creaked. She glanced back to the attendant at the gas pump, but he was talking with a customer who had come for a fill-up. Quickly, Agnes stepped inside the men's room. No one was there. She heard the steady drip of water at the sink, and went to shut the water off. Once inside, she used the back of her heel to shut the door. She didn't want to touch anything, as it all looked extraordinarily filthy. She turned the lock on the doorknob. She sighed. She flicked the light switch, but no light came on. She tried it a few times, but the room remained dark. There was some light coming from the transom, and she had a penlight in her purse, so she set her purse on the sink and rummaged in it for the light. She brought it out and turned it on. Her reflection seemed spooky with the small intense light in her hand. She looked ugly in the light.

But I'll turn into Francine, she thought, *in a few minutes.*

She set the penlight down on the sink and removed the perfume from her purse. She sprayed it in the air, but the smell of the place remained bad. It was still fairly dark, so she had a difficult time putting the makeup on.

As she was carefully applying lipstick, someone tried the door. Because she hadn't used a key to get into the men's room—the door had been left open—she wondered if the man outside would go get the key from the attendant or the manager. She grew scared. She closed the lipstick up and dropped all her makeup into her purse. She went back to the toilet stall and shut the door behind her. She would wait until the man outside went away, and then she would wait another five minutes. The toilet stank, so she had to hold her nose.

In less than a minute someone opened the door.

She saw the light on the ceiling above her as the door opened and closed. A breath of clean air whisked through the stink of the men's room.

The intruder tried the light switch. She heard the sound of water in the sink. She looked through the crack in the stall door. He was walking back. She hoped he was going to use the urinal, but instead he tried the tall door. He tried it twice. She wondered what he was thinking. Was he thinking: *Hmm . . . pretty strange that the door isn't opening considering no one else is here.* Or was he thinking: *I'd better go to another rest room, this one's out of order.* She stood there, back against the wall, holding her breath.

She heard his footsteps as he walked away.

She heard him peeing in the urinal. The flush. The door of the room opening and closing.

No sound.

He had left.

Water was still running in the sink.

She figured that she had better get out of there quickly, so she unlocked and opened the stall door and stepped out into the rest room.

He was there. He stood in front of her, blocking her way.

Agnes dropped her purse, gasping. She tried to move, but her limbs seemed to be made of stone.

She couldn't see his face because of shadow.

He said, "Knew I seen you come in here."

He reached down and grabbed her around her shoulders. She struggled against him, but he held her tight. He covered her mouth with his hand and took her over to the sink. She managed to work a hand free and slammed it back, hoping to hit him in the face. Instead, her hand went into the mirror, and she felt glass splinters. She grasped one of the glass shards and brought it up to his face and sliced across what she hoped was his ear, when she realized that she could not breathe at all, and that was the last thing Agnes Hatcher remembered until she woke up in the motel room in Las Cruces, her wrists tied together.

"Where am I?"

The man didn't look at her. He was watching TV. He said, "Las Cruces."

She began crying.

"I didn't rape you or nothin'."

After she finished crying, she said, "Please let me go home, mister. Please."

The man turned off the TV and looked at her.

She knew who he was.

He was the manager from the Mobil station. Mr. Farquar. She had known him since she was eight. He had always been the manager of the Mobil station. He said, "Can't do that."

She said nothing. Her throat was sore, and she was thirsty. She didn't want to ask him for a glass of water because she was afraid that he might do something terrible to her. She heard a fly buzzing at the window.

"It's not awful," he said. "What I'm gonna do. It's not awful."

She shut her eyes and pretended she was Francine and not stupid Agnes Hatcher.

"All I'm gonna do," he said, "is fulfill my destiny with you."

"You kidnapping me?" she asked.

"Naw. Can't call it that. But I know 'bout who you are . . . I seen it in your eyes. I know you go in the room to change so other kids'll think you're just like them.

You and I, we know each other from ways back. Centuries." He turned to point across to the window, as if behind the curtains and venetian blinds were all of human time. She noticed that part of his ear had been sliced off. *I did it,* she thought, and her heart beat slightly faster, thinking that she could really hurt him if she wanted. If only her hands weren't bound. He said, "I been huntin' you a long time."

"I'm thirsty," she said.

He stood and went to the bathroom. She heard water. He returned with a plastic cup full of rusty brown water. He held it up to her lips.

After she took a drink, he said, "Do you remember me?"

She blinked. He seemed to get angry. She was afraid he would hit her.

"You don't believe me. I'll show you who you are," he said. He set the cup down on the nightstand and sat next to her. He put his arm around her shoulders. She could smell his sour breath. He squeezed her, and she felt a brief pain as he pinched her. "Look."

As if she'd been practicing for this all her young life, she said, "My name is Agnes Hatcher. I live in Empire, California. I get straight A's."

His eyes grew wide, and then he laughed. "You bitch," he said. "You're hiding from me, I know you're in there."

He reached into his pocket and brought out a small, thin-bladed knife. He twisted her head so she was looking at the mirror that leaned against the low dresser.

(Remembering decades later, she thought she'd seen a flicker of it, of that other face.)

He brought the blade up to the edge of her forehead. It was almost a tickling pain as he began skinning her face. He whispered, "Bridey."

She screamed, but he held her head tightly in place as he continued.

The screams echoed throughout the motel court, and the police were at the room within twenty minutes.

But by that time the motel room was empty. Her abductor had already packed her into his car, and they were gone down a dirt road that led up into the mountains. It would be six years before she would see the light of day again.

Agnes Hatcher returned to consciousness, in the waiting room of Darden State, blood showering across her fingertips.

In her hands, cupped like a dark red bird,

a human heart.

CHAPTER 24

Agnes was finished with the woman named Kuehl in less than two minutes. The woman had not had time to cry out, which was for the best. Unlike Donna Howe, the woman was dead, and very quickly.

Agnes Hatcher took the car keys from the woman's pocket, and her pocketbook. The woman had a Ford Mustang key chain with a small beeper for an alarm system, forty dollars in cash, one MasterCard. Pictures of husband, children. Driver's license.

She glanced through the doors to the ward and saw the policeman speaking with one of the therapists.

She went to the double doors. She walked out through them as if she were just coming from a short visit to one of the mentally ill. She remembered a woman's walk she had once noticed, a sort of rhythm to the way she walked. She could imitate that. In her mind she pretended she was the woman, and then the walk came easy. No one would notice Agnes Hatcher. They would think it was this other woman, someone who walked with less confidence, with less direction. It took her less than three minutes to get to the staff parking lot. She passed no one on her way. It was the afternoon, and even with the police milling around, it was slow, and people were sleepy and inattentive. She held the alarm beeper high up, and pressed it twice. Two high-pitched beeps came from the left of the parking lot. She followed the sound to a blue-gray '89 Mustang. She got in, buckled her seat belt, and put the key in the ignition.

She felt the blood against her skin. It had seeped through Donna Howe's bulky dress.

It was warm like new milk.

She put the Mustang in reverse and pulled out of the parking space.

A man in a suit, probably some kind of inspector, waved to her as if he knew her. He had a gray mustache and very little hair. She thought she had seen him before once or twice.

She smiled and waved, wondering if he could see the blood on her chin. Not caring.

In her head, the one word that had fueled her in the loneliness of her captivity: *Destiny*.

As she drove away, within the walls of D Ward at Darden State, she could not know that the second body was found, Leona Kuehl's.

She could not know that the police sealed the building within minutes.

Or that Rob Fallon had confessed that the woman named Agnes Hatcher was now hiding beneath the building, in the closed-off underground chambers where once upon a time all the patients at Darden had been housed.

Agnes Hatcher knew none of this, but she was assured by her own feeling of her fate that she would reach the only man she had ever loved in time to prove to him that all she had ever done, she had done for him.

She had spent her life searching for him.

And now they would be together.

Forever.

CHAPTER 25

Carly said, "She can't get out, Trey, not with all those people around at Darden. How could she get out?"

Trey shrugged. "Any number of ways. I know her. That was her on the phone just now. With cops searching the place, all the psych techs and doctors are going to be somewhat disoriented. Some of the patients will be acting out right now because of the commotion. No one is necessarily looking for her, or they're assuming that she's somewhere within the gates. To be honest, nobody really knows what she looks like. We've got pictures of her when she came in, but her face gets covered most of the time, and she's been in ten years. She could have a disguise. Who knows with Hatcher? Instead of the Gorgon, she should've been called the Chameleon. I've seen her imitate people's voices and mannerisms almost perfectly. She can be anyone she wants."

"Call Jim. Find out what's going on."

"I just tried. The line's busy. It'll be busy for the next four hours. I might as well watch the news tonight, I'll get more information on it than I would over the phone. My assumption is that they know she's out now. The cops have probably shut down a few miles around Darden. If I were there, maybe I could do something. Maybe not. But I'm here. I'm on vacation. Dammit."

Carly put her hand on top of her husband's. She leaned against him. As if with some telepathy, he felt her warmth and love. He drew away from it. He felt cold inside.

Carly let go of him. She sighed. "She's four hours away, surrounded by cops, and she's probably more than a little disoriented. This is probably the safest place we could be right now."

"Maybe you're right. It just has me in knots, what happened. And how the hell did she get this number? What—did she attack Jim? Did she get this from the weekly log? How did she know where to find me?"

Carly raised her eyebrows. "Well, there's not a lot we can do right now. I know. Let's go for a walk, okay? Down to the beach." She stood up and went over to the dresser. She opened the top drawer and withdrew a pair of sweatpants. She slipped into these and tossed Trey a pair of khakis.

The world outside, the path down the hillside, all of it was nearly silent against the sound of crashing waves out on the rocks. Because the Fourth of July was coming up, banners had been unfurled throughout Avalon proclaiming the upcoming fireworks display on the water. Since it was still early in the week, day tourists were lined up along the docks, waiting to board the boats back to the mainland. The sun had gone beyond the far hills, but was still fairly high in the sky, casting a halo over the small town. Everything in it seemed peaceful and lazy. Carly walked ahead, wrapping her pouch around her waist, wearing flipflops and sweatpants and that great T-shirt. The smell in the air was vaguely dusty, not as clean as the earlier part of the day, brought by a slight wind from the hills. Trey took it all in at a breath: *vacation,* he told himself. *Vacation.* He slipped on his sandals, the Birkenstocks that Carly had given him for his birthday five weeks before, holding on to an old section of wooden fence for support.

"Wait up," he said.

She turned about, smiling. The sunlight created an aura around her. She drew the small Instamatic from her pouch, and snapped his picture quickly, as if afraid he would lose his expression in the next second. "Gotcha!" she cried out. She pivoted to the right and took a picture of the harbor below.

Picture this: a beautiful, happy woman, a wife and mother and social worker, caring, loving. With husband and kids. A family. Everything in the world at our feet. Life good for us. And I still can't enjoy any of this. Not completely. Trey feigned a smile, but it slipped when he caught up with his wife.

She didn't seem to notice. She took a deep, luxurious breath. "What is that? Hibiscus and—maybe gardenia? Mmm . . . let's just junk everything and move here." She grabbed his arm, shaking it. "Wake up, wake up. I want the happy-go-lucky guy back who I married. I know he's in there somewhere."

Trey pulled away from her, and then gave her a sideways hug. His forehead furrowed with worry. "If only I'd been there. I could've done something. I know more about Hatcher than the others do."

Carly, sounding slightly exasperated, said, "That doesn't matter. They'll find her inside the gates somewhere. It'll take six men, but they'll get her tied down again."

Wearily, he said, "I don't know."

"This job is driving you nuts, Trey. Don't let it."

Something in the tone of her voice disturbed him.

"I'm not going to hold it in anymore," she said.

"Hold what in?"

"This is hard for me to say."

A minute passed, and it worried him, the way she was acting, the look on her face. They were almost all the way down the path, to the main road. Somehow he knew what she was going to say.

He touched his fingers to his own lips. He pointed off to some scrub on the other side of one of the row of small cottages.

A doe stood still, watching them also.

Then it ran off into the underbrush.

"I'd like to wish the world away," he whispered, kissing her. When he drew back from Carly, it seemed as if his unhappy mood had been passed to her. Her face was etched with concern.

"You *have* to leave your job, Trey," she said.

It barely came as a shock to him, this previously unspoken demand. Yet, she looked guilty, as if keeping from saying these words was tantamount to cheating on him or abandoning him.

"Trey, I mean it. Not just think about quitting, but actually just do it. You have to leave your job, because I don't want you like this ever again. And you're like this all the time. Almost relaxed, almost here with me and the kids, but not completely. You're always part there, and it consumes you. I can't manage with half a husband, and I won't let the kids have half a father. You need to get out." Carly had never been this direct about her anger over his work. It had always come out in little jokes, or a graveyard humor about the tragedies and near-misses at Darden. Now she even looked cross. Sometimes Trey had trouble keeping things in perspective, and it got the dog up in him to be told what to do—*to leave his job, not nudged, not asked, not manipulated into leaving it, but to be directly told to leave it.*

Then he calmed down. He felt like a man defeated. She was right. He had to leave his work at Darden.

"It's funny," he began. "You get into a place like that when you're young and you think you can make a difference. You think you can actually save someone. But you can't. Not just at Darden, but anywhere. My dad was wrong. He always told me you could save someone if you kept yourself strong and prepared, but you can't. You can save only yourself."

"Oh, Trey," Carly said. "It's not that melodramatic. You can do all kinds of things. It's just that I don't want our children to lose their father because he's too tied up in the lives of criminals. I don't want to lose you either. We need our life. That place is too dangerous, and you're too sensitive. I know you're good at your work, but you need to get more out of life than just work."

They kept walking, and as Trey glanced down the hillside, he thought he saw the kids down below, near one of the ice cream parlors. Where was Jenny?

"Carly, is that Terry and Mark?"

She looked across the thin slice of the main drag that she could see clearly. "Maybe. It's hard to tell."

"Jenny's not with them," he said.

"I'm sure she's around there somewhere. Don't panic."

"We're paying her to stay right with them."

"Enough." Carly stopped in her tracks. "Nothing is going to happen to them here. See what that place has done to you? You think everywhere is like that ward. Well, it's not. Trey, you always go off like this, as if the worst thing's going to happen, as if everything has to be a life-and-death situation."

He could tell that she wished she hadn't said those words. Not exactly in that way. Not those words.

Life and death.

The white flash in the dark morning.

The gun.

The shadow against the dark.

"Sorry," she said. "I didn't mean it like that."

They didn't even have to talk about it directly. They never had.

It had happened, and then it was over.

A year ago, almost. The man had been released from Darden State because some loopy psychiatrist believed that he was "cured," but Trey had known better. The man was a sociopath named Wilson. And Wilson had told the others on his ward that if he ever got out, he'd hunt down anyone who had ever hurt him, including Trey. Trey had one nightmare after the next about Wilson, what he had seen Wilson do to people, from the autopsy photographs of the family in Long Beach. Trey bought a gun and then spent three months at a target range in San Bernardino learning how to shoot it.

And then, one morning.

When it was still dark.

The noise in the kitchen.

The fear, creeping up the back of Trey's neck.

Knowing that Teresa's room was near the kitchen.

Knowing that Wilson was loose and out to get revenge.

Trey went, shivering, with the gun, down the hall, through the living room.

In the dark.

Someone was at the back door. By the kitchen.

In the dark morning.

Trey stood in the doorway to the kitchen.

The morning light was purple.

The shadow against the dark was the exact shape of Wilson.

Trey could never be sure that he didn't rewrite his memory. Still, he felt even then that he knew that it wasn't Wilson, but he didn't care, because this was an intruder in his house.

He couldn't even remember actually drawing the trigger back.

All he remembered was the white flash in the dark.

And then, with the light on, seeing the man.

Where the bullet entered.

Trey began jogging down the path on the island, past the summer cottages, past the Zane Grey Hotel, not toward his children, but away from the memory. He had managed to stop thinking about it for four days straight, and now it was back. It had him. He could hear Carly calling for him, but he had to run. He had to do something to get the memory out of his head.

He stopped at the bottom of the road, glancing back.

Carly was walking slowly down the hill.

He felt a gulf between them, as sure as if they'd just had a fight. And the blasted thing for him was that he knew it was not her fault. He knew that he was the one to blame for being panic-stricken and paranoid and overly protective and wary and . . . frightened. He sat down on the edge of the road, curbside, his head in his hands.

He waited for his wife.

The first words out of her mouth were: "It's been a year. The guy was breaking in. Nobody thought you did anything wrong."

He didn't look up at her. He knew it was a lie. He knew that he had been what one of the policemen had called trigger happy. He knew that he shouldn't have shot the gun. He knew he shouldn't have done anything other than perhaps call the police to come around and check out the noise at his kitchen sliding glass doors.

But he was afraid. Not just of some released lunatic who had sworn a vendetta out on him. But afraid of anything that might test his courage. Afraid of anyone who might suggest that he wasn't the strong man he pretended to be to the outside world.

"Trey," Carly said as if from some great distance, as if she were on the opposite end of the world from him. "Are you all right?"

Luckily, she didn't mention the tears. He didn't want to acknowledge them himself.

She squatted down in front of him, touching his shoulder with her right hand. "It's about that man, isn't it?"

Trey nodded.

They didn't say anything.

After several minutes he got up and dusted himself off.

"It's going to be hours till sunset," he said. "I wish I were at work right now. I think I could help. Let's go find the kids."

CHAPTER 26

Mark said to Teresa, "She's gonna get in trouble if Mom and Dad find out." He was standing in his sister's shadow while she bought a corn dog. She loved corn dogs, and Mark liked salt water taffy, which Teresa was also buying for him. When she had the corn dog in her fist, she passed him four wrapped-up pieces of taffy.

"I don't care if she ever finds us again," Teresa said in what Mark thought of as her haughty-princess voice. "She's a rhymes-with-rich."

"Witch?" Mark asked, not quite getting it. He opened a wrapper and popped a taffy into his mouth. "What do you think she's doing down there?" He pointed to the alley between shops. He didn't look down it, because it grossed him out to see Jenny and that boy together. What they were doing.

"Mom says it's called canoodling, and it's something that grown-ups do. Only not on company time, and Daddy's paying her a lot to be with us. Even though

I'm too old to need a sitter." Teresa took Mark by the hand and led him over to the arcade. "I've got six quarters left. I'll give you three and I keep three. I want to play Street Fighter."

Mark liked video games a lot, but the dark arcade scared him a little. It practically had no lights inside it, except for the game machines. He didn't like these types of games either. They were all about attacking people or car races. He liked the Donkey Kong game they had at home, but he couldn't find it in the Island Arcadia World. He watched Teresa go over to the Street Fighter game. He wandered around between the machines. There were only a couple of kids hanging out there, and they seemed a lot older than him.

He decided that he didn't want to play anything. He put the quarters in his pocket and went back out into the sunlight.

Jenny was at the end of the block. He didn't want to attract her attention, so he tried to hide behind a dress display in front of a shop.

But it was too late. She saw him and shouted for him. He stepped out into the slanting sunlight. Mark began walking slowly toward her, his head down, his hands in his pockets.

Jenny quickly stubbed out a cigarette. "Where the hell have you been?" She had a look in her eyes like a crocodile. Mark thought she was pretty, especially in the eyes, but not when she was in a mood like this.

"We were waiting for you."

"And where were you supposed to wait?" she said, grabbing him by the hand and jerking him forward.

"We just went to the arcade."

She dragged him back to the arcade and got out of the sun. She stood inside, among the clanging and beeping machines. Jenny squatted down to be at eye level with him. "I'm sorry, Marky. I just was worried."

"I know. We shoulda stayed near you."

"I was just saying good-bye to Tommy. He thinks you're both real nice. Real well behaved. You won't tell your daddy about this, will you?" The pretty look came back into her eyes.

He breathed a sigh of relief. For a minute she had looked like a monster. Now all she looked like was the pretty girl who baby-sat him. "No."

"Promise?"

He nodded. He wiped his finger across his chest. "Cross my heart and hope to die, stick a needle in my eye."

Jenny Reed laughed. "That's so cute. Stick a needle in my eye. God, that's so cute. You are the cutest thing. That Terry over there?" Jenny let Mark lead the way to his sister.

When they reached her, Teresa half turned and said, "Oh, it's you."

"Listen, woman to woman." Jenny smiled. "You understand about boys, don't you?"

Teresa said nothing. On the game screen, one of the players kicked another in the head. Cartoon blood splashed out of the opponent's head.

"I left you two for only a second," Jenny said defensively.

Teresa had run out of quarters. "I don't need a baby-sitter anyway. Just because my parents think I do and hired you doesn't mean I need one."

"That's right," Jenny agreed. "You're old enough. So if your folks ask, tell 'em I ran to the ladies' room or something."

Teresa stuck her nose up at this. "I don't lie. If my

mom and dad ask anything, I'll tell them that Mark and I were fine all day long."

"Cross your heart, Terry"—Mark poked at his sister's back—"and hope to die. Come on."

Jenny giggled and then opened her purse, fumbling through it. "Look, I'll give you some more quarters."

"Hush money," Teresa said disdainfully. Then she held her hand out.

Mark knew this about his sister: She didn't lie, but she could be bribed. She liked money and what it could buy. Teresa took several coins from Jenny, and then crossed her heart to seal the bargain.

There were things about Jenny that Mark hated, and things he liked. Whenever her mood shifted to anger, she was a nightmare. But when she was like this, giving out quarters and giggling, he liked her.

"You have the prettiest eyes. They're like blue marbles," he told her. He felt himself blushing, because he sort of had a crush on her. He just wished she wouldn't smoke cigarettes or kiss that boy.

Jenny sighed. "You're an angel. And good for my ego. I'm sorry for taking off like that. I won't do it again. Cross my heart, hope to die, stick a needle in my eye. Friends?"

He nodded.

She hugged him tight.

The squeeze of her hug felt good. Even though his mother and father hugged him a lot at home, on this vacation they both seemed kind of wound up to him.

After two more games of Street Fighter, Mark saw his parents out on the street.

"Hey! We're over here!" he shouted as loud as he possibly could.

His mother grinned broadly when she looked over,

startled, in the direction of the shout. His mother tugged at his dad's elbow and pointed into the arcade.

Mark noticed that his dad looked worried. His dad looked the way Mark had felt when he was afraid to dive into the swimming pool.

CHAPTER 27

So much of life was unplanned, and yet it often seemed to work out the way it needed to. Agnes Hatcher pulled the car off the road after she noticed the patrol car behind her. The patrol car followed her into the Wal-Mart parking lot. She parked in one of the spaces but was only slightly apprehensive. *It will work out,* she thought. *It was meant to work out.* It was her first time on the outside in years, and even the air was something of a shock to her. But she had to behave as if she were the woman who owned the car. *Kuehl.* She had to behave as if she were just stopping off at Wal-Mart (a store she had never heard of before) on the way home from work.

The policeman parked his car behind hers.

Agnes opened the door and got out. There was a jacket in the backseat. Although it was warm out, she drew the jacket over her shoulders in case there was any blood on her blouse.

The policeman was lanky and young. Possibly in his

mid-twenties. He had blond hair and tanned skin. Blue eyes. He was very handsome. She wondered what it would be like to have him on a table. She wondered what she would need to remove from his body that would be his essence, his driving force.

He grinned. "You've got expired tags," he said, opening up a ticket book. "Can I see your registration?"

"You could," Agnes said, "only it's not my car."

His eyes widened a bit. "A friend's?"

She nodded. "A coworker's. I borrowed it to run out and get her some new hose. She has an important meeting. She has a run in her hose." Agnes said each word as if a man could not possibly understand this problem.

"Well. Tell you what. Tell your friend that she's three months late. She needs to get down to DMV pronto. Okay?" The policeman nodded.

She could tell that he was flirting with her. It felt cold when people did that. It felt as if they were standing too close and trying to peer inside her eyes. But she knew that it was what people liked. *It was the animal in them doing their mating dance, circling around, waiting for the moment to press their sweaty bodies against yours.*

She smiled. "You are just about the nicest cop I've ever met."

"You've met a few?"

Agnes nodded. "Uh-huh. I like cops."

"You ever go to dinner with them?"

She giggled. "Now you're embarrassing me. I feel like I'm trying to pick you up or something. And I'm not that kind of girl. And I'm far too old for you."

"I'm twenty-eight. You're in your thirties, right? Not much of an age difference there." He stepped closer, thrusting his hand out. "I'm Rick Hunt."

She shook his hand delicately. She noticed the veins

on his forearm. He was well-muscled. Muscles could be difficult, unless the cutting instrument had a sharp, serrated edge. "Rick Hunt," she repeated. "I'm Kathy. You live around here?"

"Just the other side of the freeway."

For a moment Agnes wondered if meeting this cop was part of her destiny. But something felt wrong about the moment. "Well, I have to shop and then get back to work. Can I call you? I don't really like to give out my number."

"I understand," the cop said. He scrawled his name and number across a ticket and passed it over to her. "Give me a call soon though, huh?"

She smiled. "Yes. I will."

She walked away from him, feeling more than a little nervous. He might report the car's tags to his dispatch, and Darden State might already have reported the Kuehl woman's death and the stolen vehicle.

Agnes didn't look back to see if the cop named Rick Hunt was writing anything down. She just knew that she would have to get away from this area of Riverside, California, quickly, if she was going to ever fulfill her destiny.

Inside the Wal-Mart, she found what she needed.

CHAPTER 28

"We could be twins," a woman said in aisle six of Wal-Mart.

Agnes had just picked up the Clairol shampoo-in color. She turned around.

A woman of approximately her height with shorter blond hair was grinning at her. The woman was no more than twenty. She had brown eyes to Agnes's green. She had thinner lips. She had a mole at the lower left side of her chin. She was slightly heavier than Agnes. Southern accent. She was a talker. It was practically a disease with her.

"Don't you think? I know there are a million women in California with blond hair, but look how our faces are alike. I swear, we could be twins."

"Oh, my," Agnes laughed. Her voice melted slightly into a Southern cadence. "We could, almost. Isn't that funny? And we're both from the South."

"I have a twin," the woman continued. "She lives in

Memphis. We never see each other anymore. She don't look half as much like me as you."

"Oh, Lord," Agnes said. "And me from Chattanooga."

"No!"

"Yes. I was only born there, though. We moved when I was three."

"Well, this is just too much . . . My Jerry's never gonna believe it." As the woman continued speaking in her friendly Southern accent, Agnes noticed the basket in her arms. The woman was buying makeup.

"I wish I had your skin tone though," Agnes said. "I'm old enough to be your mother."

"No," the woman said, making a gesture with her hand that seemed at first threatening to Agnes, but then she realized that it was a friendly, confidential sort of gesture. The woman was sweet, honest, sincere.

She would be easy to subdue.

"We buy the same makeup," Agnes said, nodding toward the Maybelline in the woman's hand basket. "But I need to get a good pair of scissors. My son—he's got a school project. A lot of cutting and pasting. And I need, let's see, a map. I need one of the coast."

"Really? Taking a trip?"

Agnes nodded. "My husband and I are thinking of going to Catalina."

" 'Twenty-six miles off the California coast,' " the woman began singing, and then lost the tune. "You never been there? Oh, you're gonna love it, honey. It's beautiful—and the history. That Cathedral Rock place with all the caves—my Jerry, he fishes sometimes with his buddies. He says you get the most fish early in the morning right out by those white cliffs." Something in the way the woman described the place made Agnes think it was the right place to go to.

That her Jack was there too, waiting just for her.

Knowing.

"Let's go over to the school supplies section, honey," the woman said. She grabbed Agnes by the arm, and they trotted off together. Agnes unconsciously picked up the cadence of this woman's movements: lively, syncopated, only slightly unsure. Agnes could clap out with her hands the rhythms to most people she had ever met. She could remember to the smallest detail tics and sweeps of limbs, the way a nose wrinkled at a laugh.

When they reached the appropriate shelf, the woman held up a small pair of rounded scissors. "Will these do?"

Agnes shook her head. "No. I need the sharp kind. When he's done, I can still use them for clipping coupons."

The woman laughed. "I swear, we *are* twins. Here"—she grabbed a pair of large scissors and tore them from their cardboard backing—"this'll do you."

"Perfect, thanks." Agnes accepted the scissors, holding them with the box of Clairol and the lip gloss.

"It is so nice to meet friendly folks in California. Everyone out here seems too rude."

"Ain't it the truth." Agnes shook her head.

Agnes made sure she got behind the woman in the checkout line and kept talking with her about what a coincidence that both of them should be there, and both should be from Tennessee, and both should have husbands named Jerry.

Agnes told the woman that her car was parked behind the Wal-Mart, back by the Dumpsters. "I hate leaving my car in the sun, don't you? I practically melt in weather like this," Agnes said, practicing the woman's walk.

"Don't I know it," the woman said, slapping at the

air as if fanning away mosquitoes. "But thank God there's no humidity out here. Couldn't you just about die when you think of how sweltering it was back east? Couldn't you?"

"Sure 'nough," Agnes said, slipping into a slight Southern dialect.

As they rounded the Dumpster area, the woman said, "You sure you parked back here, honey? Maybe you're round the other side."

Then she looked back, perplexed, at Agnes.

What she saw made her gasp, and she would've cried out had not her vocal cords been raggedly severed with the dull edge of a pair of scissors.

Agnes watched her hands do it, as if they needed no guidance from her.

As if what her hands were doing was natural.

Instinct.

As the afternoon grew late, Agnes parked the woman's Buick Skylark at the edge of an arroyo, out in Timoteo Canyon. She took seventy-five dollars from the woman's purse, as well as her MasterCard and American Express card. She had noticed that a few miles down the road was a bus station, but she did not know where the bus might take her, or if one came through this time of day at all. Agnes might have to hitchhike if she was to get to her destination in a timely manner. Everything was starting to work against her, she thought, after the fates had brought her so far. The woman she'd murdered had bought a Hershey bar at the Wal-Mart. Agnes, who was feeling hungry, tore into it and devoured it, feeling a little like one of the animals herself. She would have to eat later on. She needed to keep her energy up.

Then she opened the map she'd bought, folding it over until she found the island.

Santa Catalina.

She traced her finger from one side of it to the other.

She was looking for some sign from the fates that this was the right place.

An omen that both his and her unconscious minds were working in unison.

As she traced a line from the town of Avalon south and then west, she found it.

The words: *Kirk in the Rock Caverns.*

And, in parenthesis, beneath this phrase:

(Capilla Blanca, 1607, Franciscan Brothers)

She didn't need to know more than rudimentary Spanish to understand what this meant.

It gladdened her heart: *The intersection of time and space.*

Whitechapel.

CHAPTER 29

Trey Campbell kept trying to reach Darden State at the pay phone down on the docks. Carly was pointing out fish near the rocks while Mark leaned over the edge of the dock to try to see them better. Jenny sat with her legs crossed beside him. Teresa seemed a little despondent, and kept her gaze far out to sea as if nothing in her immediate surroundings was of interest.

Trey felt nothing but anxiety.

The phone line was busy for a few minutes before Trey had the operator cut in on the line.

"I need Jim Anderson," he said to the policeman on the Darden end of the phone.

After several minutes Anderson's voice came on the line. "Who's this?"

"It's Campbell."

"We had another attack." Jim Anderson's voice was weary. He had taken some Valium, probably. The way these investigations went, all employees on the ward would be held within the institution for twenty-four hours while the police scoured every inch of the compound. "Leona Kuehl. Hatcher did her number on her."

"Dead?"

"Yeah. She's luckier than Donna. Donna's so chopped up, even if she pulls through, she'll wish she were dead. The cops think Hatcher's in the underground."

"She's not," Trey said.

"Huh?"

"Listen, Jim. She called me. Just before four. She called me. Now, how did she get my number here?"

"You sure it was her?"

Trey said nothing.

"Trey, I'm the only one with your number here. She didn't get it off me, that's for sure."

"Check your pockets."

"What?"

"Do you have my number on you?"

A pause on the line.

"No."

"Did you leave it anywhere?"

Another pause. Jim said, "Aw, hell."

Trey wanted to slam the phone against the booth. "What does that mean? Does she know where I am, Jim?"

"Yes" was all Jim Anderson said.

"What the hell do you mean by that? How in God's name did she get it?"

Jim said, "Donna Howe. I gave it to her when she came on shift last night."

Trey closed his eyes. The words going through his mind were not the kind he liked to use with his wife and kids and their baby-sitter standing three feet away.

When he felt composed, he asked, "How did that happen?"

"Well, you told me to. You told me that you wanted to be on call in case there were any emergencies. You told me that if something needed doing, you wanted to be contacted so you could get back in time and fix it."

"So you wrote the number down for Donna. At least Hatcher may not know where we are exactly."

Jim coughed.

"Please tell me you wrote the number down and handed it to Donna. Please tell me you didn't—" Trey erupted into a fit of cussing. He noticed, out of the corner of his eye, Jenny taking Mark and Teresa for a walk to the end of the dock.

Sounding as if he were about to face a firing squad, bravely Jim said, "We've just been passing it back and forth. It's not like I could've predicted that Hatcher would maul Donna and then take it."

Trey whispered into the phone, "Tell the cops she knows where I am and she's coming for me."

"Don't get all bent out of shape. Jesus, she's not going to go catch the ferry to Catalina tonight."

"I know Hatcher, Jim. I know her. I'll contact the local police here. You tell the cops there that Hatcher has a vendetta with me. That she called me here. That she knows where I am."

"Don't get so bent out of shape. Rob Fallon says she's still here. Maybe she is."

"Rob Fallon is a sociopathic head-chopper. Trust me. I know Hatcher. She is going to come for me."

Jim Anderson hung up the phone on the other end.

Trey let his end dangle as he walked over to Carly.

"I wish I smoked," he said. "I feel like doing something self-destructive."

"I guess that was bad news."

"What time does Jenny get off work?" Trey asked, waving to the baby-sitter and his kids.

"Another hour."

"All right. Let's not get Marky and Terry upset. You think we could pay Jenny some overtime tonight? Special circumstances."

"We can ask. Why?"

"This woman—this psychopath Agnes Hatcher—has our cottage address and phone number, and the last time I spoke with her at Darden, which is going on ten years, she told me that if she were free, she would get me. Simple as that. Now, one more question, love of my life. Do you mind going with me to the police?"

CHAPTER 30

The police station in the town of Avalon on the island was small. There were four offices, and two jail cells in back, primarily put to use over the past two decades as a drunk tank for locals who needed to sleep it off over the weekend. There was a computer on each desk, and the woman who sat at the dispatch radio was not dressed in any kind of uniform. She had close-cropped red hair and a good figure. Her name tag read Gloria.

She was all business, however, as she logged Trey's complaint. "Okay. We've got four officers out and two in." She nodded to one of the glass-walled offices. A stout man with a crew cut sat at the desk, also not in uniform. He wore a sweat-stained white shortsleeve shirt and smoked a pipe. "That's Oscar Arboles. You can talk to him. I'll contact the mainland and see what's up with this Hatcher woman there."

Trey turned to Carly. "If you want to hang out here, I'll talk to him alone."

"No way," she said. "My *abuelita*'s father was an Arboles. Maybe we're related. And I wouldn't miss this for the world." She strode ahead of him with more confidence than he felt. He couldn't help but notice that his wife looked great, and always did in situations like this: pulled together, self-assured, a natural leader.

He tried to catch her confidence for himself as he followed her into the office.

After introductions, Oscar glanced at the blue computer screen, and then back to them. "So, you're a psych tech at Darden. My hat's off to you. And you think this woman might come here."

"Yes."

"I can't say if she's coming here or not, but she very definitely escaped. A police officer in Riverside actually spoke with her an hour ago. He radioed in a problem with this woman's car, and then when the license was traced, it was found to belong to another employee at your workplace. Leona Kuehl."

Carly reached over and squeezed Trey's hand.

Oscar leaned across the desk, holding his pipe up. "Hope this doesn't bother either of you."

"A little," Carly said. "I have asthma. I seem to detect smoke at three paces."

Slightly disgruntled, Oscar tapped the pipe's smoking ashes into a wide glass ashtray beside the computer. "I just like the smell of it. So. Tell me how you play into this."

Trey took a breath, then began. "I've studied this woman for twelve years. I was her first and only friend at Darden. I thought I could rehabilitate her in a way that psychiatrists and drugs could not. I was wrong. We became close, briefly."

Oscar looked from man to wife and back. "Intimate?"

"Not like that. We just shared a lot. I felt there was

a human being lurking behind the woman who, at that time, was called the Surgeon. But I was wrong. She's a machine. She fell in love with me, to some extent. And then, when I saw what she did to try to prove her love . . ." Trey closed his eyes, remembering. The attack on the other inmate. The old man who hit Trey hard in the face. Agnes Hatcher had known about that, and when she had the chance . . . "She operated on another patient," he said as matter-of-factly as he could. "Nothing fancy. Just a botched lobotomy. That was when she went back into heavy restraints and heavy sedation. The orderlies covered her face most of the time too. They called her the Gorgon because of the way she looked at them. She looked at everyone as if they were bugs to be studied before they were squashed."

"Except for you," Oscar said.

Trey nodded. "With me she felt we had a shared destiny. She couldn't understand my betrayal of her. She told me that she would find a way to wake me up to who I was inside."

"Mr. Campbell," Oscar said, leaning back in his chair. "That's not the most dangerous of threats."

Trey kept his cool even though he wanted to explode. "I have worked with sociopaths and psychopaths and murderers and torturers since I got out of college. Agnes Hatcher isn't the same. She's a machine. She has no feelings, even for herself. All she has is a constant motion toward. Getting to me is one of her primary goals."

Oscar shrugged. "Let's assume she does come for you. There's an all-points bulletin out for her arrest. Within the next hour everyone in Southern California will see her face on television. We already have an officer who saw her. We know what car she's driving. She's going to be caught. It would take her six hours at the earliest to get here. You and your family are probably safer here than anywhere else in this state. We don't have murders in Avalon. It costs too much to get here if you're just out to kill someone. This woman is already slipping up. She will be caught soon."

"Maybe I should talk with one of your colleagues instead," Trey said.

"He or she will say the same thing," Oscar said. "But don't get all twisted up about this. If you like, I can have another officer escort you home and stay with you at your cottage. Or you might consider checking into one of our local guest houses for the night. That way, if Agnes Hatcher manages to elude the police on the mainland and find a way out here after the last ferry has gone, and finds your rental, at least you won't be there."

"That's a terrific idea," Carly said, looking at Trey. "We can stay at the Breakers, there's a nice pool there for the kids. That way, you can get some rest tonight."

"I guess I'm overreacting a little. That's a good idea, officer."

"Oscar. No Arboles, no officer. Oscar. So"—he turned his attention to Carly—"how did you end up with a gringo like this?"

Carly half smiled. "All the good ones were taken."

On the street again, Trey said, "I hate that word gringo."

"It's not the best one." Carly threw her arms around him. "My big baby."

Trey shrugged her off. "He was patronizing."

"And you are paranoid." Carly stopped in her tracks. "Maybe this woman is out and maybe she's dangerous, Trey, but you are on vacation. We can just check into a hotel for the night if you're that worried. I'm not. I think that crazy woman is probably out on the desert right now or up in Big Bear. Catalina is too hard to get to. Oscar's right. Maybe she could get over here tomorrow, but the chances are, they'll have caught her by tonight. Let's go pack up and get a room at the Breakers. And quit playing the victim.'' She stepped around him and went out to the end of the dock.

When Trey got there, she was sitting next to Teresa, braiding her hair and then unbraiding it. Mark sat at the edge of the dock, near the pylons, with Jenny, who was pointing out boats in the water.

When he saw his father, Mark leapt up and went running over to him. ''We saw the funniest movie, Daddy. And I saw a shark.''

Teresa corrected him. ''It was a dolphin.''

''It was big,'' Mark said.

Trey tousled his son's hair. ''I'll bet it was.''

''They come out of nowhere,'' Mark said enthusiastically. ''It's really cool.''

Jenny laughed and swiveled around to face him. ''They were a handful.''

''We appreciate your staying the extra hour.''

''Time and a half,'' she reminded him. She rose up clumsily. ''Mark's got a little cough. Not much of one. I don't think it means anything.''

''Hijito,'' Carly said, reaching her arms out for her son. He trotted over to her, and she hugged him. ''Cough for me.''

Mark smiled. He coughed twice.

''Oh, he's dying.'' Carly raised her eyebrows to Teresa. ''Your brother's dying from too much fun.''

Mark laughed, and Teresa smiled.

Trey grinned too. It was okay. Nobody was coming after him. *Agnes Hatcher will be caught within a few hours.*

Or she'll hide out on the desert. This island is the safest place for us right now.

This was confirmed after he'd walked Jenny home to her parents. Trey jogged back to the cottage, and Carly greeted him with "Agnes Hatcher is dead."

CHAPTER 31

Carly had taped one of the news broadcasts for him, as she sometimes did when he worked double shifts at home. It was habit. Oddly enough, the mayhem of the world often relaxed him. She rewound the tape to a certain point and pressed the play button on the remote control.

A KCBS reporter was standing in front of an arroyo. "The body of serial killer Agnes Hatcher was found three hours after her escape from Darden State Hospital."

A photograph of Agnes Hatcher flashed on the screen.

It was an early one, from her first entry into Darden.

It was how Trey remembered her.

Then the video switched back to the reporter. "Hatcher was found at the base of this arroyo." The video switched again to a lighted canyon, with a burning car. "She was dead on the scene. Local police told this reporter that the vehicle she was found in has not yet been traced to an owner, although it appears to be a Buick Skylark. Hatcher was the notorious cop-killer of Pasadena, who, in 1981, known as the Surgeon by Southern Californians . . ."

The reporter kept talking, and Carly said, "See? All that worry for nothing."

Trey replayed the video three or four times before he could convince himself that Agnes Hatcher was indeed dead.

"This calls for a celebration," Trey said, clapping his hands together. Then he stopped. "My God, I can't believe I said that."

"I can. She sliced and diced, what, twelve, thirteen people in her career? You were like this when Jeffrey Dahmer died too. Don't start feeling bad for people like that," Carly said. "I'll make the drinks."

"No, it's just that Agnes was different. She was a machine, sure. But she never really had a chance. Probably she was already something of a sociopath when she was tortured as a child. That's all it takes though, some kind of torture. It's as if as kids they had this dark spot in their brains. Someone, usually an adult, takes the time to just step on the kid over and over until that darkness blossoms into a flower. Until it becomes the only thing they know. The only thing *she* knew. It's a mystery of life why it happens exactly like that. But it's no mystery as to where it came from."

"There are a lot of abused kids in the world who don't grow up to operate on unwilling victims," Carly said. "There are a lot of kids who get stepped on, and they go on to run companies or become social workers or write novels. They don't all murder for fun."

"That's part of the mystery—why does one do that and the other become a Gorgon? Where's the place where it happens? Maybe only reincarnation can account for that kind of personality, coming out of nowhere. Maybe it's not nature or nurture. But we know she was tortured for many years of her life. I think half of what she did was to try to make other people feel the way she felt on the inside. She just did it the wrong way."

"That's putting it mildly," Carly snorted. "Well, I'm jubilant that she's no longer of this earth, sweet psycho queen that she was. So, are we going to have wine or margaritas?"

"Maybe later," Trey said. "I have to watch this video again. To drive it into my skull that the Gorgon's destroyed."

CHAPTER 32

Agnes Hatcher sat between the old man and his young grandson in the backseat of the station wagon. The younger man, only in his mid-thirties, who was the boy's father, drove. The wife, in the front seat, hadn't liked the idea of picking up a hitchhiker at all. But Agnes had given them gas money, and so she had proven honorable enough for the grandfather who sat beside her. It was the only car to pick her up in forty minutes. "All the way to Los Angeles?" the driver asked.

"Yes." She smiled. "My boyfriend Pete's meeting me. We're going to see *Miss Saigon.* I really appreciate the ride. If my stupid clunker of a Nissan hadn't broken down, I wouldn't've had to bother you. I hate the idea of hitchhiking. Haven't done it since I was nineteen."

"No bother," said the husband in the front seat. "The holy spirit told us it was okay to give you a ride. We're going to a revival downtown."

"Really?" she said.

The wife eyed her in the car mirror. "Have you met Jesus yet?"

"Oh, I think so," Agnes said. "Many times." She turned to the blond boy beside her. "What's your name?"

He looked up at her with weary eyes. "Timmy."

"You're a very well-behaved young man," she said.

The grandfather tried to touch her knee, but she pulled away from him.

"Jesus is our savior," the husband said. "Let me tell you a little about him."

Agnes Hatcher closed her eyes and wished that they would go away. It would be a few hours until she got downtown, and then another hour to San Pedro. When she would arrive there, she'd finally dye her hair and change her look. She was exhausted. An hour or two of rest wouldn't hurt. Perhaps she could sleep while these animals in the station wagon droned on about their religion. She had a fantasy about slicing each one of their throats, but there were too many of them together.

After all, she needed the ride. She had followed her inner voice, the one that led her hands to slice the nice Southern woman back by the Dumpsters at Wal-Mart, the one that told her to use the nice Southern woman's body as her own decoy. The voice that guided her without words, just the vibrations of the universe. It had all been promised her from the past life, he had told her. *"With these lives, with this blood, we consecrate our own eternity together."*

The voice had led her to the arroyo, led her to stuff the oily rag into the Buick Skylark *(the oily rags in the oven, surrounding her beloved,* memory threatened). Led her to burn the woman's body, the seats of the car, the slow smoldering fire that caught.

Then, using the natural leverage of the slight rise in the arroyo, she pushed the Buick ever so gently, and it rolled, burning down farther into the wasteland.

The voice within her let it be known that this would make the others leave her alone.

Let her follow the trail of instinct to her most beloved goal.

But the voice had died down when she'd had to accept the ride. She had stood at the bus stop for fifteen minutes when the car had pulled up to her. It was fate, she could tell. And with these Jesus sellers all around her, driving her to Los Angeles, she wished the voice and instinct would guide her hands to stop up their mouths permanently.

But it was silent in her head.

She had no choice but to play sweet and kind and compassionate.

Next time she intended to take the bus.

CHAPTER 33

At the cottage on Catalina Island, Mark Campbell was determined to overcome his fear. He slipped out of his flipflop sandals and treaded out to the patio. His mother was inside, teaching Teresa some guitar chords—Teresa played the piano a little, but was new to guitar. His mother had been taught classical guitar when she'd been a girl, but she was teaching Teresa some basic stuff like "Puff, the Magic Dragon." Mark considered that "girl time" between the two of them. So now he figured it was "boy time" between him and his father. He stood a few feet back from the edge of the pool, and then turned around.

"Daddy?"

"Marky? What's up?" Trey was sitting in one of the lounge chairs nearby, watching the night.

The last gasp of day, almost an aura of pale lavender light, played about the edges of the undulate hills that rose behind the cottage. The scents of honeysuckle and jasmine wafted on a light breeze. Night was like a cloud, pushed from the east, toward the hills. It was so close to being dark that it felt like it was past Mark's bedtime. Only his parents were letting him stay up later than usual because it was a vacation. His father seemed lost in thought. Mark felt his father worried too much about things.

Mark shifted his balance from one leg to another nervously. "Will you help me?"

Trey sat up in his chair. He leaned forward. He was a tall man, so when he leaned like that, he seemed to stretch and almost reach where Mark was standing. "With what?"

"I want to dive."

"Now? It's getting late. How about tomorrow morning?"

"Well," Mark said, slipping his T-shirt over his head. "You always say 'Better late than never.' "

Trey chuckled. "That's true."

"I've been thinking how I've been a 'fraidy-cat. And it's dumb. It's dumb because Teresa can dive. I'm just scared when I look in the water and see me staring back. But with the lights out, I don't see me in the water. It's just water."

"You sound too logical for your age," Trey said, mussing up his son's thick, dark hair. "Okay. I'll get on the edge with you." Trey unbuttoned his shirt, tossing it on the chair as he rose. He unbuttoned and unzipped his pants, stepping out of them. He wore blue boxer shorts. Mark laughed out loud and pointed at them when he saw them.

"That's not your swimsuit." Mark's eyes went wide. "It's your wonderwear."

"Them's my swimmin' trunks now. Okay, what you do is . . ." Trey went to the edge of the pool, leading

Mark by the hand. He leaned forward, his arms all the way forward too, palms flat. "Pretend you're like a dolphin. Push with your feet, press with your hands."

Mark imitated his father's position beside him. "I'll fall."

Trey said, "You won't. You'll dive. And you know how to swim, so once you're in, you just swim. Let's both go at the count of three. Okay?"

Mark nodded, but felt uncertain. He leaned forward and closed his eyes so he wouldn't have to see how far the water was from him.

Trey counted to three, and Mark pushed with his feet and pressed with his hands. He did a bellyflop and sank down into the water. His stomach burned, and it was so black around him, he didn't know which way to turn.

He swallowed water, and thrashed around, until finally his father grabbed him around the waist and brought him up.

"Marky, Marky, it's okay, it's me, are you all right?" Trey said, lifting him up to the side of the pool.

Mark coughed. He was crying, and felt like a baby. "I can't do it right," he said. "I get too scared."

Trey hefted himself up the side of the pool and out of it. He went to get a towel. He brought a big striped one back and wrapped it around his son. "You did fine," he said, sitting down beside him on the concrete. "Let me tell you a little trick I do to get through difficult things."

Mark leaned his head into his father's chest. "What's that?"

"I use the as-if rule. The as-if rule states that if I don't know how to do something, I act as if I do, and then it works."

"Like pretending?"

"Kind of. But it works because it's not quite pretend.

It's something that our minds have within us already. It's already in your body and brain to dive, Mark. You're half fish as it is. Look how well you swim."

"Yeah. But I can't dive."

"But act as if you can. Nobody can do anything until they work at it. But if you never try it, you'll never do it. Sometimes I do things I didn't think I could until I think of the as-if rule."

"So I'm supposed to act as if I can dive? But what if I crack my head open?"

Trey grinned, rubbing his shoulders with the towel. "Then you act as if you meant to do that. Want to try again?"

"Really?" Mark asked. "I'm almost dry. Won't Mom get mad?"

"I don't think so. Not if you're learning something new. Here"—Trey pulled the towel off and stood up, holding his hand out—"if we keep trying till you get it, you won't be afraid tomorrow and you can show off."

Mark took his father's hand. "I might still be afraid."

"Oh, yeah. I'm afraid sometimes when I dive too. But fear is there to help protect you, so you'll think about how to do it safely. Let's give it one more try." He took his son over to the pool's edge.

"As if," Mark said, leaning forward toward the dark water.

"As if," his father repeated.

"Are you afraid of anything, Daddy?" Mark asked solemnly.

"Everyone's afraid of something, Marky. We have to overcome fear to face whatever it is that we're running from. We have to live as if we're brave."

This time Mark did a good dive, and came up, dog-paddling toward the pool ladder.

"Know what?" he asked his father.

"What?"

"I don't have to be afraid of nothing no more."

"That's right. Not grammatical, but still correct."

"Know what else?"

Trey shook his head.

Mark climbed up the ladder to the concrete. Then he leapt over the edge, cannonballing, making a huge splash when he landed. When he came up giggling and sputtering, he cried out gleefully, "That's what!"

CHAPTER 34

The woman with the neatly trimmed reddish-brown hair, wearing jeans and a light blue cotton sweater, glanced around the oyster bar. This was the sixth dive she'd entered along the waterfront that evening. It stank of fish, and even urine from the open men's room door. It was only eight P.M., but already the place was packed, wall to wall with people drinking beer or devouring oysters and shrimp. The place was filthy, although the management had tried to cover this up with sawdust on the floor and dim lighting all around the bar and tables.

It reminded her so much of her past, of the very reason she was there.

In an ordinary saloon, or restaurant, no one would look twice at this woman. Her hair was an obvious over-the-counter dye job. Her eyes were pretty but small. Her face was pale, as if she hadn't been in the sun in years. Her lips, thickened with glossy lipstick, were curved nicely. She would be considered moderately attractive in another setting.

But in that particular bar near the harbor, she might be the most ravishingly beautiful woman in all creation.

There were seven men sitting at the bar itself, and when she entered the bar area, four of them turned to look at her. The others slowly turned also when they noticed their compadres doing so. She tried to read them, but it was difficult with the noise from the jukebox, and all the talking. She had been to three other such bars already, and was exhausted. It took a lot out of her to get a good reading of someone, particularly in this sort of environment.

One of the men winked at her. He was twenty-two or -three. Five o'clock shadow. Dark, thick hair. Brown eyes. Well-built but short. His eyes stayed on hers the longest. She counted the seconds until he looked away. Then he glanced back again.

Boldly, she walked over to stand by him.

"Hi," he said. His breath was spit and beer. He was horny. That was enough.

"You'll do," she said.

"Huh?"

"You got a boat?"

He nodded. "Sure. Me and a hundred guys down here. Why? You into boats?"

She felt chilly, and was afraid for a moment that someone else was watching her. Someone who was threatening in some way. She felt that way whenever one of her own species was nearby. She could feel whoever was watching her just as if they were touching her face. She didn't particularly like that feeling. It passed, however, and she returned her attention to the man on the barstool.

"Yeah," she said. "I really get into boats."

She turned slightly to the right, but could not tell where the threat was coming from.

When the dark-haired man ordered her a beer, she knew.

It was the bartender. *One of us.*

A former surfer boy. Blond, six feet, well-muscled, pre-melanoma. His hair was cut short and flat on top, long and stringy on the sides. He was not handsome at all except for the athleticism of his body. He had pale blue eyes. Crow's-feet about their edges. He was still, the way an animal being hunted was still. The bartender glanced at her, and she knew that he was one of her kind. He was reading her as much as she was reading him.

They didn't have to say anything.

When he went down to the far end of the bar, she followed him.

"Do you have a boat?" she asked.

He nodded. He kept his hands in the pockets of his yellow shorts. She assessed from his bad posture that he was weary. He had possibly been doing speed for a couple of days. He would need to wind down. He said, "I can get a sailboat. Do I know you from somewhere?" His voice was raspy, as if he'd spent years raking it with razors.

"I don't think so. I need a boat with a motor. It doesn't have to be very powerful. Can you help me?"

"Sure. They call me the Cobra." He thrust his hand out to shake hers.

She didn't return the gesture.

That was all it took. His shift was off by midnight.

Off-shift, he wore a Hawaiian shirt that was blue with

blotchy yellow flowers over the black muscle shirt he'd worn at the bar. He kissed her as soon as she stepped up to him outside. His kiss was dry. He smelled like whiskey and Old Spice aftershave.

She stepped back, away from his kiss.

"I thought you liked me," Cobra said.

"I do. Not like that."

"Okay, whatever."

"The boat?"

Cobra cursed under his breath. He walked ahead of her, then stopped and half turned. A nearby streetlight cast a pale glow around his form, like a halo. "I swear we met before."

"Maybe," she said. "Do you believe in past lives?"

He answered her with a laugh. "My VW's around the corner. I can take you to my buddy's boat. Where you headed?"

"Catalina," she said. She stood beside him and watched the darkness as if she expected something to attack her. Yet she did not seem afraid. Just wary.

"Tell me another one." He smiled good-naturedly as she caught up with him.

"All right," she said. "If you won't take me there, I'll find someone else. There's always someone else. But I can give you something you've never had in life before."

"Yeah? What's that?"

"Fulfillment."

Then she reached up to his face, holding it in the palm of her hand. She knew what the animals wanted. *I will train you, dog, and you will understand your place in life. I will lead you to where you need to go.*

She kissed him, and held him there for several moments.

"I thought you didn't want that," he whispered.

"Now I do," she said, feeling her eyes glazing over.

Feeling her *mind* glazing over too. "In this alley. Against this wall."

She pulled the sweater over her shoulders and head. She leaned back against the cold bricks. She moved out of her body, to a vantage point above them, as if she were not the woman below at all. She watched the animals bite and kiss and explore each other's bodies.

Then the lightning of time and space struck her, and its flash erased all memory of the present life.

October was a month of rain that year. A constant beating against the roof far above, and leaking down into the crawl space where she slept. She slept too much, but she was too weary afterward, after what she and her lover did, to do anything else. She awoke when a rat scurried across her leg. She crawled down to the opening, into the coal storage room. He was beating at the door again. Beating so hard, she thought he would break it down, or call attention to their nest.

She couldn't let anyone else know about their nest or it would be all over.

She was sure that even her neighbors, if they knew what she did there with him, would set them both on fire inside it.

She glanced at the great oven, with its twin doors. Remembering a childhood fairy tale of a witch being thrust inside it by evil little children. Of being baked alive by evil children.

All children were evil.

She didn't like to think of the times she'd had to sleep in that oven with her lover, doors shut. Just to keep from being discovered, mashed in together, as if they were one person and not two. Hearing the hounds and the whistles as the coal basement was searched. Feeling his hands about her . . . Thinking of the children lighting the fire in the oven, laughing as the witch burned.

She hoped that he would take her away from there, as he'd promised.

She prayed that they could use the lifetimes they'd collected to fly away.

He was, after all, a gentleman. And she would be his lady.

She stooped down, pushing open the small door. He was there. He grabbed her, dragging her into the night. His kisses were like poison, for she felt herself die with each one.

He cupped his hands against her breasts, squeezing gently, then more harshly. The gaslight was dimmed in the fog and drizzle, and she could hear the clatter of horses as the carriages went by on the street. She smelled garbage and sewer runoff. Rats squealed at the doorway to her left. She had never been so cold and so hot at the same time.

She felt her blood burning within her, and she wrapped her legs around his waist.

He had the most beautiful face she had ever seen. It was like a pagan god's, wild and ravishing and golden.

"Do it," she moaned. "Do it."

He took the small scalpel and touched it against her breastbone.

She met the cold metal and pressed herself against it.

The blood was warm, and he brought his face down to it, tasting it.

He kissed her lips, passing her blood back to her.

Rain began to fall, and she heard the others, in the alleys, among the tenements, their cries of lust, their tender moans.

Lightning cut across her vision.

"You a vampire or something?" Cobra asked. He touched the side of his neck and examined the blood on his fingers. "I dig vampires. I tasted blood sometimes. That was some love bite you gave me."

Agnes Hatcher's eyes came back into focus.

She was in the wrong skin. It was the wrong place. She wanted to be back there, back with her beloved, back with the only man who truly understood her.

She wept for all she had lost over her lifetimes. Cobra held her tight.

His friend's boat was small, just a sloop with a nine-horsepower engine. It had a single cabin, with two narrow sleeping bunks, and a hot plate and bathroom. They kept the sail tied to the mast and used the motor.

Agnes Hatcher fell asleep in the cabin. When she awoke, it was still not morning.

The boat was docking on the island.

She felt his power, his pull. *Jack. Beloved.*

Cobra wanted to fall asleep, but he was too keyed up. He told her how much he loved her. He confessed his crimes: the stolen things and the murdered people. He murdered like a child, from a quick temper. He loved like a child too.

"Do you love me?" he asked.

"No," she said truthfully. "But I knew all about you when I saw you. I knew what you had done."

"I saw it in you too," he said, nodding off to sleep. Agnes knelt beside him and watched the dreams come to his closed eyes. Then she went up on the small deck and waited in darkness.

The threat of memory enveloped her, not her beloved, but the man from her childhood:

The man tying her to the chair, carving into her skin with the wood-burning iron. Teaching her about the life they had been a part of. Teaching her about how he had been there, had witnessed what she and her lover had done in the previous existence, and he had taken her in order to punish her for what she had done.

After days of the torture, the memories of the past life had come so strong and vividly that she could not see the present world for the past one.

The past life exploded across her vision: She was nineteen, and living on the streets of London, occasionally sleeping in the great sweatshop basements, which were warm at night, even though the machines clattered all through the dark hours. She had been forced into the life at twelve, by her mother, and did not enjoy any man's touch, no matter how much he paid.

Then, one night, she met the gentleman surgeon. He promised her more than money. He promised her immortality.

"Each life we take," he whispered into her ear as he made love to her, "we gain another. The ancients knew this. That was their reason for human sacrifice. I have taken several lives. If you will believe in me, I will never abandon you."

She had delighted when her lover scarred her, or drank a drop of blood from the tip of her finger. He had a hunger to consume life in every way. He taught her how to use the surgery tools, how to peel flesh back so as not to traumatize it.

They took the other girls together. She held Mary Kelly's head down while her lover operated. She watched the terror of their victims' faces, and finally the love too, for in suffering these whores achieved a great beauty. She watched for the police, or she sat in the carriage, waiting for him to run out swiftly so they could drive off.

Her life was never the same afterward. It was full of gorgeous moments, of the taste of blood, of the understanding that the immortal soul was in the body itself, in the part of the body that was most important to its owner. Sometimes their victims lived in their hearts, and sometimes in their genitals and sometimes in their brains.

And always, afterward, he brought the scalpel to her to taste. He would combine their bloods: their victim's blood, and then hers, and then his.

Communion for eternity.

She took the scalpel from his hands. She pressed it lightly against the thick skin of his collar.

His eyes burned with excitement. She could tell that he was aroused in a way that he had never been before.

She brought her face to his and kissed him as a man kisses a woman, hard and deep and conquering.

"We are the gods," he said after the kiss.

That was the day of the hounds.

That was the day of the coppers with their shouts and fury.

That was the day of betrayal.

That was the day she opened the locket that was pinned inside his cloak.

As the sun rose slowly from the east, behind her she saw its first purple-pink rays slash the island.

There it was: the place of her dreams. Not the squalor of a district of an ancient city, but the reincarnation of that place in their new time, their new skins. It was sacred to her now, this island.

This island was the place where time and space would meet.

The great spires of rock, ending in needlelike formation. The several mouths of caves, stacked on top of each other. The bottom, an opening into its depths. The magnificence of it in the early sunlight, where its white chalk seemed to glow against the rest of the island. It rose like the Gothic cathedral of nature.

The sacred home of the fates.

Capilla Blanca.

CHAPTER 35

It was on the morning news, but Trey and Carly both slept late the next day, so they missed the item.

It was on the radio, but Carly had it turned to a Top-40 station.

The woman in the canyon was finally identified as Mary Beth Clark, born in Tennessee, a resident of San Bernardino County for the past eight years. Although much of her body was burned, it was the eye color that caused the discrepancy with Agnes Hatcher. Eventually Mary Beth's husband, Jerry, contacted the police about his wife, and all of it was traced back to the Wal-Mart in Riverside.

Trey Campbell awoke at nine-thirty, innocent of this correction in the news. He was feeling like he had the biggest hangover of his life.

CHAPTER 36

Which he did, because when he and his family had gotten back home the previous evening, and after Marky's now-famous perfect dive in the pool; and after the kids stayed up to watch *The Little Mermaid* again, he'd made a couple of killer margaritas. Heavy on the Cuervo Gold. Light on the sweet and sour. Crushed ice. *Heaven.*

And had drunk them both because Carly wanted a glass of wine instead.

They'd stayed up until two watching bad late movies. Then he'd begun reading *The Three Musketeers,* which Carly had brought. He couldn't put it down until about three-fifteen. He fell asleep on the couch, and when he awoke, it was because Mark was spritzing him with water.

"What the—" he gasped, wiping at his face with his hands.

Mark was giggling. Already in his swimsuit and wet, he held the plant spritzer up and sprayed a few more times. "It's only water!" Mark began dancing around, until he dropped to the carpet, exhausted.

Carly was out on the porch sipping coffee; Teresa was taking a shower.

"We already went swimming, Daddy. I dived six times. Just like a dolphin. Now get up," Mark said with some authority in his voice.

"Look, fish-boy, Daddy's feeling a little creaky today." Trey slowly rose up, tasting the aftereffects of the margaritas mixed with morning breath. He stumbled to the bathroom and shuddered when he saw what seemed to him an old man staring back at him. After his shower he felt like going right back to sleep.

But Carly had an idea.

"Oh, no, nothing special today, please," he groaned.

"Just listen. We'll call Jenny and cancel today and take the kids horseback riding. Won't that be fun?"

Mark cried out, "Yeah!"

"I'm an old man, sweetheart. My ticker ain't so good." Trey faked a limp and hunchback.

"It'll be fun."

"Okay, okay, but let's not cancel on Jenny. Mark's too young to go on a horse."

"I am not!" he protested.

"Are too. Nobody in their right mind is going to rent a horse to a kid your size, trust me."

"Discrimination," Mark said, and the word seemed too big for his mouth.

Trey looked at Carly. That would be a word that he'd heard her say. "It's because you can get hurt on a horse. Until you've had lessons . . ." The worst thing about telling his son this was that Trey knew that he sounded just like his own father. He had always hoped he'd grow up to be a more liberal, easygoing dad, but it just never happened.

"Terry hasn't had lessons," Mark said.

Teresa appeared at the patio doorway. She dripped water from head to toe onto the stone walkway. "I don't want to ride horses. They're filthy."

"What?" Trey said. "Every girl likes horses."

"Not me. Why can't I stay here and swim?"

Carly sighed, clapping her hands together. "Okay, okay. Your father and I will go riding, and you guys hang out here. You're sure you want to do that?"

Teresa nodded, and padded back to the swimming pool. A loud splash in the water signified her approval of this plan.

Carly ran out to the pool, shouting, "But you are not to go swimming without Jenny watching you. Get out of there right now."

Mark looked cross. He eyed his father like he was the enemy. "I don't wanna."

"What can I do to make you happy?" Trey asked.

Mark furrowed his brow. "Take me riding."

"No can do. What else?"

"I don't care." Mark, who moments before had been in a good mood, got up from the floor and stomped off to his bedroom.

"You knew he couldn't go riding," Trey said after Carly came back inside.

Carly crossed her arms. "Don't jump on me just because you're tense. Why don't we just do separate things today? You go do what you want, which I'm assuming is get wound up, and I'll go horseback riding."

"I'll go, I'll go." Trey rolled his eyes. "I didn't mean for this to become a production. I'm not jumping on you. Okay?"

"All right. And it'll be fun. You wait and see," she said.

The one piece of advice his father had given him that

seemed to work in his marriage, the only decent piece of marital advice the old man had ever conferred upon him, was: "Remember, son, the wife is always right. You remember that and you'll have many happy years ahead of you." It seemed like the code of the troglodyte to believe that, but Trey had found that it worked. When he and Carly got in a jam, he generally gave in and told her she was right. Things often worked out from there.

Jenny arrived at ten-thirty, looking like she'd just come from working in a garage, which was not her normal look. "I forgot to wash my clothes," she said by way of explanation. "These were the only things even approaching clean in my dresser." She twirled around in the dungarees and bleach-spotted blue chambray workshirt.

"Like we care," Trey said cavalierly.

Jenny's face lit up when she heard about the horseback riding. "Oh, God, it's so great. If you can get Elmer to let you off the trail with his old nags, you can ride out to the beach around the coast. It's so pretty. Just make sure you go to Elmer's. Tell him I sent you. God, I wish I was going."

"Thanks for the advice," Carly said, bringing Jenny's traditional morning cup of tea to her from the kitchen. "Sorry you can't. It's just that the kids . . ."

"I know, I know. Kids are always falling off horses around here. It's amazing to me that some parents let them ride at all. I've been riding since I was ten, but I took lessons the whole time," Jenny explained to Mark, who sat right next to her. Trey could tell that Mark had a crush on the baby-sitter, and would probably cry when he had to leave her at the end of the week. Jenny turned to face Mark and pinched his cheeks. "Hello, you cutie pie. What do you want to get up to today?"

Mark's face went from fascination to disapproval. "I want to go riding."

"We can go hiking," Jenny said. "You like that?"

"Maybe. If I was on a horse."

"Well"—Jenny winked at Carly—"we'll pretend."

Outside, Carly grabbed Trey's arm. "Jenny has a major crush on you."

"Naw."

"When you were outside with Terry, she told me she thought I was the luckiest woman on the face of the earth."

"You're kidding."

"No. Really." Carly leaned against his shoulder like a schoolgirl. "Of course, I set her straight."

Of all the horses in the stables, Trey was given the one nicknamed Assassin. And there was a good reason for it. It kicked several times just being brought out from the stables. He had a time just getting the saddle strapped on tight so it wouldn't slip off out on the trail.

"Why is it you get the horse named Dorothy and I get Assassin?" he asked as he tried for the third time to get the saddle on the large dappled mare.

Carly grinned. "You can handle her."

"I haven't ridden for six years. She's tried to bite me twice already. My rear end is going to be burning soon from the friction, and she'll probably drag me in the dust for several miles. Come on," he groaned, finally getting the horse to breathe in long enough to strap the saddle on sufficiently tight. He grabbed the horn, slipped his right foot into the stirrup, and raised himself up to the saddle. "Just stay still for about a minute, okay?" Trey started giggling like a kid.

"What's so funny?" Carly asked, her back straight as she trotted her mare up to his.

"I was wondering what she's called for short, Ass?"

"Get your mind out of the gutter. Call her Sassy."

"That's cute. Sassy. Hey, Sass, ya wanna gallop?"

"Trey, no, no," Carly said.

But it was too late. Sassy was galloping across the sloping hill, and, in turn, Carly's horse started up too, even though its rider kept calling out, "Whoa, whoa, slow down."

It became one of the best days that Trey could remember, between his horse trying to bite him even while he was astride, and the riding across the beach, at the water's edge. More than loving Carly, he liked her like he had never liked anyone before. He thought: *It's nice to be married to your best friend.*

Trey thought such warm, loving thoughts right up until the time Assassin threw him into the waves, and between the fear of breaking his back and the fear of drowning, he cursed his sorry fate.

Carly rescued him in due course, and he spat seawater out of the side of his mouth. "No bones broken," she said.

He sat in his wet clothes in the surf and watched the mare take off on its own down the beach. "Great," he said. "Now I'm going to have to chase down that damn horse."

CHAPTER 37

Jenny was doing something very bad, Mark was sure. He knew that even though she was a lot older than he was, she shouldn't be pouring the wine from the fridge into a glass for herself. But he said nothing.

He had just finished lunch, and Teresa was out by the pool, taking a nap in the sun. Mark was bored, and even though Jenny had told him to stay outside because she'd be right out, he had come back in.

"What's wrong?" Jenny asked as she sipped from the glass.

"Huh?"

"You're looking at me funny, Marky. What's up?" Jenny wore what Mark would call a phony grin. It was the smile he usually had when he lied to his parents (and was caught, as usual).

"I know what you're doing," Mark said slowly. "And you're not supposed to."

"This?" She held up the glass full of wine as if it were

a soda. "Oh, we grown-ups are allowed. I already asked your mom."

This threw him. If she had asked his mother's permission, then it must've been all right. He didn't pursue the subject further. She got sillier as she drank the wine, and picked up the phone and spent half the day yakking it up with her friends.

Between calls he said to her, "I liked you."

"I like you too." Her words slurred together.

"I mean I used to like you." He wrinkled his nose up, his eyes squinting. "I don't think you're very nice."

"Marky, Marky. I know you don't mean that." She leaned over to give him a hug, but he pulled away from her.

"I do too." He crossed his arms on his chest.

"You're still mad because you didn't get to go horseback riding."

"Am not. I don't care about dirty old horses. I'm telling my parents."

"You'd do that to me?" She took another sip of wine. The phony grin had disappeared. She looked like she was about to pout.

"Yeah. I would." He nodded. "You're being bad."

"Well." The tone of her voice changed dramatically into a nasty, low tone like a cat that was about to scratch. "How would you like it if I made up stories about you and told them? Who do you think they'd believe?"

"That's mean. To make up stories."

"You'd do it to me," she said.

"I'd tell the truth."

"Listen," Jenny said, flipping her hair back behind her shoulders. "You're too young to understand these things. If you want, tell your parents. But that means they'll get a really nasty baby-sitter. Ugly and big and mean. There are only two of us on Catalina."

Mark considered this for a moment.

Jenny picked the phone up again and tapped in a number.

Mark got off the couch and wandered back outside. He stood over Teresa, who was sleeping on her stomach in her one-piece with ruffles at the edges.

After a minute she woke up. "You're dripping on me," she said.

"I don't like Jenny."

"Me neither. That's why I didn't want to go anywhere."

"Mom and Dad like her."

"That's because she fakes everything around them, like she's Miss Perfect. I can see right through her. If they knew why she wanted to take us to the movies . . ."

"Yeah," Mark said, remembering the boy that Jenny had met there, and how they had sucked face through all of *Pocahontas.* Although, it had been something of an education for him. He was curious as to why her boyfriend had kept sticking his tongue in her mouth. Mark had found it disgusting to watch. He squatted down on the concrete beside his sister. "We should run away."

"Not," she replied sarcastically. "Besides, where would we go?"

Mark shrugged. "I have five dollars."

"How'd you get five bucks?"

"I been saving," he said smugly. "Every week, fifty cents for cleaning out the cat box and feeding the fish."

"You save your allowance? Mine's gone before I get it. You've saved that money for ten weeks?"

Mark nodded.

"Five bucks can buy us ice cream," Teresa said, sitting up, doing a quick mental calculation. "And we can get some corn dogs. You wanna?"

"Huh?"

"Run away. Not very far. We can get some supplies with your money and then hide out in town. If we see her, we can just duck around the corner. Then, when Mom and Dad come back home, we can show up and tell them all the nasty stuff she does."

"I don't want to be a squealer."

"Okay, I'll do the squealing."

"But the only other baby-sitter's big and ugly."

"So what? You expect Mary Poppins? I just don't like Jenny. I thought you were in love with her though, so I kept my mouth shut."

Mark sighed. "I was. I thought she was nice. But she's naughty."

Teresa got up. "Let's go. But we have to be sneaky about it. We don't want 'the witch' figuring it all out and stopping us."

As they snuck out the back gate, Mark heard Jenny on the phone.

"Tommy?" she said. "Sure. Yeah. No, really. I got the whole place to myself. Come on over. Hey, how often does a chance like this come around? No, no, they're real little. I'll pop *The Lion King* on the video player and shove some cookies in front of them. Really private. Yeah. Just you and me and a choice of bedrooms."

CHAPTER 38

"Let's explore," Carly said, pulling at Trey's hand. They had managed to catch the errant horse, and now both animals were tethered to some scraggly trees off the riding path. The road from Avalon was below them, but it was cut off near the high rocks because of a mudslide that still had not been completely cleared from the unusually heavy rains of the late spring. Half the hillside there was difficult to navigate because of the way the rocks had fallen.

Trey glanced up the side of the hill. "All the way up there?" He turned and caught a glimpse of one edge of Avalon. They had come around the island far enough to barely see anything but the tip of the town.

"Sure," his wife said, letting go of him and running up the thin trail ahead. It led to the caverns that tunneled back to the sea. He had hiked this area with his father when he'd been twelve and thirteen, on vacation then. Carly stopped halfway up the hillside to read the sign. " 'The Kirk in the Rocks,' " she said. " 'Where the Spanish monks lived in solitude from 1605 to 1620. It became known as *Capilla Blanca,* for the white chalk cliffs on the ocean side. Enter at own risk.' You want to risk it?"

He caught up with her. "I always wondered how this place got a nice Scots word like 'kirk,' when it was used by Spanish monks."

"It's the way of *Los Estados Unidos,*" she replied. She led the way, weaving between boulders and brush, until she came to the mouth of the cavern. A large chain-link fence had been erected there. "I guess there's no risk involved here. Wish we could get in. Smell that? It's bat guano."

He leaned against the fence. "My dad and I used to come up here. He knew all the trails through this. There's a carved-out room where the monks slept. He used to take me there and tell me ghost stories."

"Nice nightmare material."

He laughed. "They were more funny than scary. He was a complex man. He drank. He could be a bully when it came to getting his own way." Trey's voice seemed to die down like a sudden gust of wind that was over. Quietly, he said, "But he was a good father in other ways." Then he brightened, as if the good memories were coming back. He spread his hands out as if creating a canvas for his memories. "He could be amazing too. He told great stories. He was cheap—really cheap. When I was in college he sold all my old furniture from home. I came back the first summer, and I didn't even have a bed." He could smile at these memories now, from the distance of years. Suddenly, another memory hit him. One he didn't savor. He remembered the old man at the kitchen door of the San Bernardino house.

Trying to break in.

The gun firing.

The look on the man's face, the gray hair, the shabby clothes.

"I wish I had never killed that man." Trey went and glanced through the fence, down into the chasms and paths of the cavern.

Carly leaned against the chain-link fence. "It was an accident. Of course, you wished you didn't. He was trying to break in. We had three break-ins in that house. I'm sorry he died too. But it wasn't your fault. Get over it."

Trey shook his head. "I don't think I can. If only I hadn't bought that gun. I was just too paranoid."

"I know you were. With good reason. That inmate, what was his name? The one who had escaped. Watson?"

"Wilson," Trey sighed. "Just like Agnes Hatcher. I assumed he would come for me. I assumed I would be his target. I guess I was wrong on both counts."

"It's a moot point in Hatcher's case, now that she died in the crash." Carly went over, slipping her left hand across the back of his neck. It felt cool where she touched him. "It's okay, Trey. It'll all be okay."

He barely heard her voice. "Looking at that old man, lying there, dying. Dead. It was like watching my father die all over again, only I pulled the trigger."

A silent moment passed between them. He felt the cool of the shade from the nearby rocks and trees. He smelled the fresh salt of the sea below them. The soothing heat that rose, incongruously, from Carly's cooling hand at the back of his neck.

"When we get back, I want you to go to a counselor to deal with this," Carly said gently. "I love you, I love our life together, but you have obsessed on this long enough. Between this and your job, part of you is numb.

I don't want my children growing up with a father who's numb in that part."

"What part is that?"

Carly took a deep breath. "The part about forgiveness. Of even yourself. Now," she said, turning so that he couldn't see her tears, "tell me the legends of the bat cave."

He began to recount for her tales of the passages around the cavern, the stories his father had told him, the lives of the order of monks who lived in silence among these chalk walls. He told her that he knew most of the trails, because his father had led him through each one, showed him the Great Room, where the monks had created their small chapel. "The statue of the Virgin Mary was in one of the recesses in the room, and it was long gone, but they'd painted the walls like a chapel, with the stations of the cross and angels and all kinds of things on white. It was really beautiful. It's too bad you can't go in there anymore. I guess graffiti taggers might ruin it."

Carly sighed. "I wish we could see it. Don't you think we could sort of break in somewhere? If you know all the trails, there must be another entrance."

"That might not be too smart," he said. "Some of those trails weren't even very sturdy when I was a kid. And there're these big drops, like wells, down hundreds of feet. Besides which, I don't think it would be a really good example to our kids if we were caught breaking in, do you?"

"Oh, it'll give them something to remember us by for years to come." She grabbed his hand, tugging. "Come on, we don't have to go in too far. Just a little ways."

CHAPTER 39

"Who are you?" Cobra asked.

"I'm you."

"Me? I don't get it."

"I know what you hunger for."

"You mean, what I done before? The killing?"

"More than that. The pleasure in it," she said.

Cobra and Agnes Hatcher had spent their morning washing up at the beach showers. Cobra sunned on the beach while she walked among the shops, hoping to catch a glimpse of a familiar face. She brought him a lunch of hamburgers and french fries. She ate nothing. Her hunger was not for food.

By the time Trey and Carly were riding, she was asking a local Realtor about rental cottages. She was shown several photographs, and given direction if she wanted to walk around the town by herself and look at them.

About the time Agnes found the exact location of the cottage she was interested in, which would be available the following week, Trey was thrown from his horse two miles away.

When she and her newfound friend trudged up the road to the cottage, it was late afternoon.

CHAPTER 40

"It's not dark at all," Carly said, leaning against the cavern wall. A shaft of afternoon sunlight cut from above and to the side. It lit most of the craggy rocks, and they could see all the way over to where the white chalk walls, which were smooth, began. They had climbed around part of the bent chain-link fence, obviously where local kids had been doing it for years. The cave was silent except for the sound of waves crashing against its rocks, far below.

"I'm telling you, we shouldn't be doing this," Trey said. In spite of his own warnings, he was leading, every now and then reaching back to touch Carly's hand to make sure she was staying balanced. The trail was not particularly narrow at this point, but at its outer edge there was a fifty-foot drop into another cave.

"This is fun, Trey. This is like being kids." Carly tried to pass him, but when she did, he pressed her back. "Sneaking into a cave that's off limits. It's like playing hooky."

"One at a time." Trey thrust his arm out so she couldn't go around him. "I don't care if it seems like there's room to walk side by side. All it would take is for your foot to slip . . ."

Carly huffed. "We've hiked trails up at Big Bear more narrow than this. Give me a break."

"The difference is, if we fall here, no one can come immediately to help us."

"You are such a stick-in-the-mud," his wife said. "So, where's the room?"

"The Great Room? I'm not sure we can get there from this trail. Maybe we can look down on it."

She pushed lightly at him. "Well, let's go."

After taking a few wider trails into dead ends, Trey finally got the right one. The light from above, where the caves opened up at the top of the hill, was growing weaker. The sun's light was shifting.

As he walked ahead of Carly, he almost stepped over the edge.

The trail ended abruptly.

Although he couldn't see them, he could smell the bats—this must be where many of them congregated. He glanced at the ceiling of rock. He could see their huddled, shadowy forms. He pointed at them to his wife. She gasped.

He whispered, "No loud noises, please. Nothing's worse than having a hundred bats swipe at you."

She nodded.

He brought her to the edge of the trail, where the rock dropped into a chasm.

The feeble sunlight descended where he pointed, and then seemed to grow brighter.

"There it is," he whispered.

* * *

Below them, a round chamber of pure, almost glowing white.

"It's not all chalk. Some of it's other minerals."

"It looks like baking soda," she whispered, mindful of the bats. "How do you get down there?"

"You don't get down, you get up. There's a trail that winds from the water level upward."

There were drawings of figures all along the white walls. It was hard to figure out from above what exactly they were, but Trey had seen them from the chamber's floor when he'd been twelve.

He said, "They're the stations of the cross. And see? In that recess? There's the Queen of Angels."

"I guess the paint faded over the years."

"It was probably really colorful when the monks were here. It's weird how I feel comfortable in here. Maybe it's all those hikes with Dad. I've never been scared in this place. It's so . . . beautiful," he said for lack of a better word.

"This should be some kind of national landmark," Carly said.

"I think they tried that. They just couldn't keep the kids from writing over it. Look." Trey pointed toward the far wall of the chamber.

Scrawled across a carved religious saint, the words CHERYL AND ROBERT 4-EVER.

"It's still so beautiful." Carly hugged Trey. "It's like our secret garden."

He kissed her forehead. "Now, let's get the hell out of here before these bats wake up."

"Wait. What's that in the middle?" She pointed downward.

"It's just a drop. It's not a well or anything. But the

monks used it to raise and lower supplies from boats. Back then the Spanish could get little boats into the water-level caves. They'd raise food and fresh water up in animal skins tied to ropes."

"You mean those monks never left?"

"Not until they died."

Carly shook her head. "That's so weird. It's like they were the anchorites of the island." She shivered and turned back on the path. She ducked to avoid an overhang, and then stubbed her toe and let out a brief but powerful cry.

Trey reached for her, and brought them both down against the floor of the trail.

The noise disturbed some of the bats, who flew as if stampeding the air over their heads, brushing Trey's back. He lay on top of her.

"Sorry," she whispered. "Stubbed my toe."

"The hazards of cave hunting," he said. "But now that I have you like this . . ." He kissed the back of her neck.

"Between you and the bats, I don't know if I'm ever safe." She pushed him off her and he rolled back against the rock wall. "Let's get out. That whole monk thing has me feeling kind of creepy."

Out in the open again, Carly said, "I feel like I've just come out of some ancient tomb."

"You have," Trey said. "When the monks died, they buried themselves at different places in the caves. Like catacombs."

"And what about the last monk?"

Trey affected a bad Boris Karloff accent. "Maybe he's still in there, waiting."

CHAPTER 41

"No," Jenny said, pushing herself up to a sitting position. "I'm not going all the way." She combed her fingers through her hair. All the buttons of her blue shirt were undone. Still, she had kept her bra firmly fastened despite her boyfriend's best efforts. She felt heat inside her, the kind that she would've liked to burn with, but she knew that boys like Tommy didn't respect girls that went all the way. No matter how blue his balls got, and no matter how much sex might clear up his acne. He had even told her that he thought masturbation was a sin, so if she gave in to him, then she could save him from sin.

Tommy lay on his back. His shirt was off, but so far he had kept his swimming trunks on. He was definitely cute, but she didn't intend to get a reputation in Avalon for him. The town was too small, and everyone would know in no time flat. She'd end up like her older sister, unmarried and pregnant at seventeen. Not in her plans.

She was going to marry a guy like Mr. Campbell, who would take her places. A guy who would treat her right. Not like the local townies. Jenny Reed was going to get off this island and go to Los Angeles. She was going to maybe wait tables until she got some parts in movies. She was going to be famous . . .

"If I begged?" Tommy asked.

She laughed, buttoning her blouse up. "Not if you proposed marriage."

They were on the bed. They'd spent part of the day getting drunk, the other part making out and grinding against each other. She was winding down a bit from the wine, and figured she'd better fill the wine bottle up with some water so the Campbells wouldn't notice that any of it was gone. Glancing at the clock, she cried out, "Holy shit—they may be back soon. It's almost three. Get up, get up."

"I'm up," he said, laughing. "That's the problem, I've been up for the last two hours."

"You are so crude," Jenny said. She leaned over and kissed him on the forehead. He tried to pull her down again, but she resisted. She pushed him away.

Jenny slid to the edge of the bed and stood up. "I'll get you one more beer, and after that you have to leave. They never get back much before five, but you never know. Remember, if they surprise us, you're twenty-one."

"It's what my ID says." Tommy propped himself up on his elbows. "Where are those rug rats? I ain't heard a squeak outta them for hours."

Standing in the doorway, trying to look sexy by balancing on one hip, Jenny said, "They ran away. But I think I saw Marky sneaking around the backyard a little while ago."

"Some baby-sitter you are."

"Hey, you get what you pay for. What's going to happen to them here? As long as I don't hear either one of them swimming, they'll be fine. I think they're just getting their revenge for you being here."

"Maybe they're watching us. Maybe they're learning all kinds of things," Tommy said, grinning.

"Like how to be drunk and stupid." Jenny arched her eyebrows, mocking him. She turned and padded barefoot out to the kitchen. She checked the road from the small kitchen window. A few tourists were bicycling by. There'd be a million of them come the Fourth. They'd come in droves on the morning of the Fourth and stay through the weekend. It was always like that when the holiday was midweek. But no sign of the Campbells.

Jenny opened the fridge and grabbed a Rolling Rock bottle from the back.

A sound behind her startled her.

"Tommy," she said, turning. "Don't sneak up on me like that."

But it wasn't Tommy.

CHAPTER 42

Teresa held tight to her little brother's hand. He knew to keep quiet because the man with the tattoos all over his arms and back looked scary. The man's shirt was in his hands, and he wiped it across his stomach and chest to get rid of all the sweat that was shining on his skin.

The tattooed man was stepping carefully through the French doors of the patio, into the cottage.

Teresa whispered in her brother's ear. "Maybe it's another boyfriend. She has a lot of them."

Mark wished his sister would keep quiet. He didn't want that man coming over and finding their hiding place. He was sure it wasn't a boyfriend of Jenny's because Mark was positive he saw a small, slightly curved knife in the man's right hand.

Then he saw the pretty woman in the jeans and sweater. She was already inside the house. He thought he saw Jenny too, but he wasn't sure.

He heard glass break from somewhere inside.

Then he thought he saw something that made a shower of red water come out of Jenny's face, and it scared him so much, he peed in his shorts. He couldn't help himself—he held tight to Teresa's hand and jumped up, drawing her with him.

The woman in the house looked out across the patio.

She moved swiftly. Mark thought it was like the nature film he saw once where a lion went after a gazelle.

She was coming for him and his sister.

CHAPTER 43

Teresa screamed, "Run! Marky, run!" She tugged at his hand, but his body was hard as stone. Mark couldn't move. Something about the pretty woman coming toward him had made him feel terribly cold. He felt like he wasn't even in his body, but was looking down at himself. At himself and the lady who moved so fast, it was like she was running, only it was more like she was bounding toward him. He wondered why he couldn't make himself go. His feet felt like they were sunken into the concrete of the pool. He tried to scream at himself from inside his head to move, but nothing happened. Even his lips couldn't move.

Teresa pushed at him and went running. There was a break in the hedge behind the cottage that led to another street. Mark couldn't even turn around to see if that's where his sister went.

Mark didn't feel he could budge an inch. He was

frozen. He tried to tell his body to run, but nothing moved.

He wished his sister had stayed with him, but she was scared too, and she would get help.

The woman came to him and leaned over. Her face was inches from his own. He could smell her sweet breath.

She put her hands on his shoulders.

She looked deep into his eyes, as if she were looking for something else inside him.

"You're his son," she said. Her voice was light. "You look like your father. You have his eyes. You have beautiful eyes."

There was blood on her teeth.

She brought her lips to his forehead.

CHAPTER 44

Agnes closed her eyes, still kissing his son. Tasting the fear on the boy's face.

Lightning thrust a spear into her brain. She was pushed into the past body.

Her head throbbed with pain as she opened her eyes again.

She was there, in the nest she shared with Jack.

Looking at the locket that had been pinned to his cloak.

Seeing the picture inside it. The lock of hair.

The woman with the dark hair and pale skin.

She went to the corner of the room to gather more coal.

All she could think of was betrayal.

All she could think of was that he had betrayed her for all eternity.

Something wild and uncontrollable was released from deep within her.

It was as if a sleeping beast were awakened.

PART THREE

CHAPTER 45

At six P.M., Trey sat alone on a bench outside an ice cream shop in town while Carly got a scoop of peppermint ice cream on a sugar cone. They'd wandered the hills and rocks, avoiding any humans they happened to spot. It had been their day to be completely alone together. He was happily bored with the early evening. Bored and still a little hungry even after they'd gotten a couple of burgers an hour before.

It seemed that the entire town was overrun with tourists at this point, and he attributed this to the fact of the Fourth of July celebration coming up the next day. His backside ached from riding, and the top of his forehead was bright red from the sun. Carly got her cone and walked down the block, window-shopping.

He could see the docks and beach from his seat, and was mildly surprised to see a medium-sized powerboat with the letters L.A.P.D. stenciled in white on its navy blue prow.

Several cops got off the boat and walked up the docks.

Carly came over and sat down next to him. "I spy with my little eye a hat and some sandals that I want to buy."

Trey pointed to the dock. "Look what I spy."

"Oh. Cops on vacation?" she said, fanning the air. "God, it's hot."

"I wonder what's up."

"Well, it's not because the dreaded ax murderess is after you."

"Now I feel bad," he said. "She's dead. Poor thing. She never had a chance in life."

"Neither did her victims. Remember that next time you feel sympathy for a sadistic killer." Carly had a way of expressing herself that always seemed to override whatever mood he was feeling. He appreciated that about her.

"It's hard to understand that kind of mind, how it perceives things. She was kidnapped when she was barely Teresa's age. She was tortured by this insane person. For years. She was almost seventeen when she finally broke free, but it was too late. She had murdered the man who had abducted her. Who could blame her then? He had tortured her, skinned her in places, kept her in a basement, chained like a dog. Taped her constantly. Bled her with small, sharp knives. And he created a monster himself in her. He had turned her from a girl with some problems into a creature from nightmares. She had a fairly unique pathology, which her abductor had apparently tortured into her. She believed that she was reincarnated, living through the problems of another existence, and that this drove her to be who she was."

"So, who was she?" Carly asked. He could tell she was trying to lighten things up a bit; her tone was facetious.

"Cleopatra? Anastasia? The Iron Maiden of Nuremburg?"

But he couldn't even raise a grin. It all seemed so sad to him. He had always felt that none of the patients at Darden were really to blame for their situation. It was as if the ancients were right: Some were born under unlucky stars. "She was a girl, also named Agnes, who lived in London around the turn of the century. A prostitute."

Carly seemed genuinely interested. "How much of her file did you see?"

"I didn't. Her psychiatrist kept that under lock and key. Agnes Hatcher told me all of it. She believed that everyone from her current life also played a part in past incarnations."

Carly's jaw dropped, in mock drama. She touched his wrist, leaning toward him. She whispered, "You were one of her past-life clients?"

Trey finally grinned. It did seem a little funny to him. *Quit taking yourself so seriously all the time.* "Not quite. She believed I was the reincarnation of her lover. He was quite a character. A man who tortured her and degraded her, but who understood her. A man who taught her about life."

Carly was silent. Then she said, "It sounds nuts, but I'm actually slightly jealous. And I don't even buy the reincarnation thing. Do you?"

"Do I what?"

"Believe in reincarnation?"

Trey laughed. He glanced toward the beach, with its last stragglers still swimming or having evening picnics. "I really would hate to come back to earth and have to figure it all out all over again. But I do. A little."

"I married a heretic," Carly said. "A recovering Cathoholic like me."

He stood up, stretching. He looked back, above the shops, to the western sky above the hills, the rays of the sun still glowing. "I'm not talking about any orthodox reincarnation theory, just the one that goes, you know, you die and then grass grows from your grave and some animal eats the grass, and so on . . . you know, the 'no energy is lost' theory. Fragments of what we are remain." Trey felt a little exasperated trying to put this into words, since he was never sure of his exact belief system except in the most general terms. Since Carly was a lapsed Catholic, religion came up in their lives only when the kids were baptized and when the in-laws visited.

Carly brought her legs up on the bench, crossing them in a pseudo-yoga position. "I'll be sure to remember to save on your funeral, then. Maybe I'll use you as fertilizer to plant some grass in the backyard. How did a nice Episcopalian boy from Riverside ever develop such independent thinking?"

"It's just a sense. It seems logical to me."

"So maybe you *were* Agnes's lover. We should go to one of those regression therapy hypnotists sometime and find out. Maybe I *should* be jealous," Carly said, knitting her eyebrows in mock worry. "Maybe she's being reborn even as we speak, and in ten years some kid will come up to you and say, 'Hey, I'm Agnes.' I'll be jealous through eternity."

"Well, you won't be jealous when you hear who her lover was."

"Queen Victoria?"

Trey laughed. "Not even close, except maybe by family ties. Apparently you are married to the reincarnation of a nice man named Jack who used to knife the odd hooker."

"Jack the Ripper?" Carly's eyes widened. "I wish I

had never asked any of this. Yikes. She thought you were Jack the Ripper?"

"Her immortal beloved. I even had nightmares for a while back then, she described it so vividly. She believed that I brought her into 'the life,' and then tried to destroy her. She told me that one day I would remember the Great Betrayal and then we would be united. One of those nice past lives."

"The Great Betrayal," Carly said. "Sounds like the Great Room those Spanish monks had." Then she snapped her fingers. *"Capilla Blanca."* Carly's eyes widened. "What a coincidence."

"Huh?"

"Capilla Blanca—the original name of that Kirk in the Rocks place. It means 'white chapel' in Spanish. Whitechapel was the area of London where Jack the Ripper did his dirty work. Isn't that weird?"

Trey caught his breath. "Yeah, it is. Very. But then again, Britain is an island, and we're on an island, and Jack the Ripper killed in Britain . . . so, oh, my God, we've both been on islands. What's really weird is that you know where Jack the Ripper stalked his victims. Maybe you were there too. Maybe *you're* Jack."

"Don't mock me, bucko," Carly said, "or you won't get any kisses. I just think it's weird that the day after she gets killed, we're walking around a place called white chapel. Maybe you *are* the Ripper reincarnate."

CHAPTER 46

"It feels like it never gets dark here," Trey said. They walked hand in hand along the promenade. The shops were all closed down, but a few of the restaurants were just serving dinner. "When is it going to get dark? I'm tired of daylight."

"Since you're calendar-impaired, I'll remind you that it's July, and we've passed midsummer night by only about a week. That's why it's not dark yet," Carly said. "Try back in a couple of hours."

"Oh. Right." He grinned.

"Hey!" Carly said as if she just got the greatest idea in the world. "Let's take the kids out tonight." She paused, dragging him with her, to examine a menu on the wall by a small bistro. "If Mark's gotten over his pout for the day, maybe he'll behave himself for some paella or . . . mmm . . . this looks good. Scampi. That's what I want." She sighed. "God, that was a fun day."

"Yep" was all Trey said. "I am a lucky son of a gun."

He took her in his arms and kissed her. Closed his eyes. Blocked out poor, dead Agnes Hatcher. Blocked out Darden State. Blocked out everything but the here and now.

For variety, they walked the narrow side streets up the hill, cutting over within several houses of their rental. The entire town of Avalon seemed silent, which matched the balmy weather. On the way back to the cottage, Trey noticed two policemen standing at the edge of the road. He and Carly exchanged glances.

"Don't get paranoid," she whispered, taking his hand. When they strolled near the two men, one of them held up his hand.

"I'm afraid I'm going to have to ask you to stop. We have an investigation in process," one of them said.

"Excuse me," Trey said. "Has there been some sort of accident? There seems to be a lot of police out tonight." Carly leaned against a fence post to tie the laces of her tennis shoes. The sky was becoming overcast, which for most of Southern California in July was unusual, but not among the coastal islands. The clouds didn't necessarily herald a storm, but perhaps there would be scattered showers that would come and go quickly. Noticing Carly, and the sky, and the policemen—these were his last moments of feeling safe in the universe.

The short cop said, "As a matter of fact, there has been something of a mishap. Do you live up this road?"

"We're renting a cottage. Right at the end. Number 224."

He knew before they even said another word. It was in their eyes. He felt his heart rate accelerate suddenly, and he broke out in a cold sweat. He couldn't even bring himself to look at Carly. He was afraid she would feel it too. The fear. As if it were a living, breathing

thing that he let out of its cage only when there was nothing to stop it.

Trey knew.

He knew in a gut-wrenching way, and before they could stop him, before they could speak, he was running up the road, toward the house, thinking only:

Let them be safe.

Please, God, let them be safe.

Let our children be safe.

CHAPTER 47

Later, it seemed like a nightmare. It seemed like the cottage was on the sea, adrift. Tables, chairs, walls, all seemed to rock slowly back and forth. His vision was limited, as if he were looking through a dark tunnel. Trey fought his way past the police. They were a blur of blue uniforms and gray suits. A woman in a black skirt and white blouse had a small Baggie in her hand and was picking something off the floor with a pair of tweezers. A policeman made a grab for his arm as he stumbled across something on the floor—he couldn't bring himself to look at the thing he was afraid might be a human body. He heard shouts as if from underwater. The living room seemed to rock back and forth as if it were being slapped with waves. His body moved faster than his mind, for he couldn't understand why there were so many policemen standing at the edges of the kitchen, using brushes and penlights on the counter.

He felt dizzy, and was afraid he would fall—but he

held on to his consciousness, his sanity. He worked as hard as he could to be strong as he ran down the hall, calling their names as if expecting each to be in the bedrooms of the cottage.

Trey felt somewhere deep inside himself that whatever was happening here, God would keep his children safe. Children didn't deserve for anything bad to happen to them. Nothing like what he was afraid of.

He kept his mind racing, keeping the flame of hope alive.

Until he saw the spray of blood across Mark's bedroom wall.

CHAPTER 48

It wasn't Mark or Teresa in the bed. It was the body of an older boy. Even this was difficult to determine. Trey felt sweat break out all up and down his spine. He began shivering uncontrollably. It was as if he had stepped into another dimension of existence. As if he had stepped into hell.

Trey's mind was wiped clean, then, for the next several minutes. He took in the room with his eyes. He saw what there was to be seen. But his brain short-circuited, and he felt very cold. He felt for an instant as if he himself had the mind of the killer. As if he were stepping into the room, seeing the boy in the bed.

Seeing the terror in his eyes as the boy beheld the knife.

The curved knife held high and brought down in a slicing motion.

The ripping of skin.

The smell, from somewhere distant, of soot and mildew. The sound of clattering hooves on cobblestones. Beating of rain against shingles. The taste of blood in the back of his throat . . .

A human being lay on the bed, his skin sliced down the middle and peeled back, stuck with tacks to the bed. His face had been completely skinned. It was a mass of red pulp.

A cop turned around when he saw Trey and said, "Who are you?" He had something that looked like some bloody body part in a large plastic bag. The evening sunlight through the long bedroom window cast a kind of rainbow across the bloodstained wall. The lampshade by the bed was spattered with something that had once been part of a human being.

Trey felt a stab in the back of his head, as if just seeing this hurt so much that he was about to lose consciousness.

On the wall, fingerpainted in blood, the word:

BELOVED

CHAPTER 49

Trey crumpled in a heap to the carpet. He closed his eyes. *Please God don't let Marky or Terry be hurt. Please let this be a dream.*

Down the hallway, he heard Carly cry out. He stood up on shaky legs, grasping the door frame. He saw her, down the hall. She was calling for their children.

Trey marshaled what little strength he had and went toward the sound of her voice as if it were his own heartbeat. He wanted to hold her until they were one being, together. Until there were no more tears, only warmth. Only comfort.

When he found her, among the cops, she was shivering. He wrapped his arms around her. He held her as close as he could get. Normally, he would feel her warmth. Now all he felt was ice.

"Trey," she wept against his shoulder. "My babies." Trey's mind couldn't focus on any one thing. Random and scattered images flashed through his mind: *Mark when he took his first brave dive, Mark when he was a week old, lying in the old Beatrix Potter blanket in his bassinet, Teresa at her fourth birthday party, Teresa dancing on her grandfather's toes when she was six, the time when Carly miscarried . . . Images of Dr. Balantine, the psychiatrist, his scalp sliced open, the blood on Agnes Hatcher's face, the look in her eyes, at him, when she cried out, "Beloved! My only love!" The image of Agnes Hatcher, face covered, in her restraints, in the steel-doored room at Darden State . . . chess games, sitting across from her and trying to figure out how she would move her chess pieces . . . walking with her in the garden, and hearing her stories about her last incarnation with him . . . his babies, his little children*—he couldn't block the images—*torn as if a wild animal had dug its claws into them.* His thoughts: *It can't be Agnes Hatcher. She's dead. I watched the news. It's what was reported. She couldn't have done this.*

A familiar voice, behind them, at the French doors to the patio, said, "My men have been looking all over for you two."

Trey glanced around. Through his own tears he saw Oscar Arboles, pipe in mouth, shining with sweat. He was coming in from the pool area with a dark-haired woman. The woman had a camera in her hand. She would be the crime-scene photographer. She had a look on her face as if none of this blood spattering the room was anything out of the ordinary.

Oscar looked as if he himself were hoping this was all just a nightmare from which to be awakened.

CHAPTER 50

"Your son is unharmed," Oscar Arboles said. He was wearing a very sweat-stained blue suit, the collar of his shirt undone, his tie askew. He was on the patio, walking Trey and Carly around the pool. "Your daughter ran down to get help. She's doing fine. A neighbor a few doors down called us. The murderer didn't hurt your son. It was that woman from the asylum."

"Agnes Hatcher?" Trey said, feeling confused. "But she's dead." He knew even as he spoke the words, he knew she was really alive. He'd known as soon as he'd run up the road to the cottage.

He'd known as if he had some psychic link with Hatcher herself.

Oscar stopped pacing. "Mr. Campbell, she's very much alive." Looking at both of them, he drew a handkerchief from his breast pocket and handed it to Carly. "We received a report of a sighting of Hatcher at a harbor saloon in San Pedro. She was seen in several places, speaking with men at the bar. She found one too. We've got him."

"We saw on the news that she died," Carly interjected. She blew her nose into the handkerchief.

Trey cussed a blue streak. "I should've known. It wasn't her, was it? It was some victim of hers."

Oscar nodded. "She's very clever."

"Clever? She's a genius." Trey cursed silently to himself. "How could I leave my kids alone like that?"

Carly asked, "Can we go to them now? I want my babies." Her eyes were filled with tears.

Oscar nodded. He went inside and spoke briefly with one of the investigating officers. When he returned, he said, "Let's go out the back gate. No use getting upset all over again walking through that . . ."

Carly clung to Trey the whole way back to the police station.

When Carly saw the state that Mark was in, she began weeping loudly. She went to him, hugging both him and Teresa. "Thank God, thank God, oh, thank you, God." Teresa was doing fairly well. According to Oscar Arboles, their daughter had not witnessed too much. She had tried to get Mark to run, had pulled and pushed him, but he hadn't budged. So she had just taken off, assuming that if she got help quickly enough, nothing bad would happen to her brother.

Teresa hadn't known what was wrong with Mark.

"A mild catatonia," Oscar said. "It happens sometimes. An event is so traumatic, the individual freezes. He'll be fine in a day or so."

Trey picked his son up and held him. Mark's chin rested against his shoulder. Trey had never in his life seen a sadder-looking boy. His eyes were all dark and seemed to have sunken into his face, becoming smaller. His lips were thin, and in a tight line. He said nothing. He reacted to nothing.

Teresa began crying, and Carly held her. Carly and Trey looked at each other. For a moment her look stung. Trey didn't know if his interpreting her expression was just his own guilt for not being with the children, or if Carly was genuinely angry with him for having the kind of job that would bring with it this kind of monster.

Oscar said, "Although there's a good chance Hatcher's already off this island, I want to get all of you off-island tonight. I'll have a couple of the mainlanders—cops—take you to Long Beach in a motorboat in half an hour. We can get your son to Long Beach Memorial for observation, but I'm certain he'll come through with flying colors by morning."

Too numb to speak, Carly nodded.

Trey said, "What did Hatcher do up there?"

Oscar was silent. After a few seconds he said, "She lived up to her various nicknames. Not a tale to be told in front of children."

Neither Trey nor Carly could leave them yet. Trey set Mark down beside his mother. He held Teresa for a while, smelling her breath, feeling her heartbeat. He wanted to stay with them. They were a unit, not to be separated. He felt like an animal protecting its young, for he wanted to guard them for the rest of their lives. He deposited Teresa with her mother and put his arm around Mark. Trey just wanted the warmth to pass through all of them. He didn't want to ever leave their sides again.

Oscar Arboles said, "Why don't we go talk in my office, Mr. Campbell?"

Carly nodded to Trey. "I'll stay here. Don't worry. We're fine." A strange relief was in the air between them. Almost an electrical charge. It was that monstrous human emotion of survival—self-survival. Two teenagers had been murdered brutally in the rental cottage, but they were part of another world of tragedy. In this world of his own family and of happy endings, Trey felt as if he and his family were lucky. They had been spared that horrible tragedy. They had somehow skirted it. Days later he and Carly might be back at their home in Redlands, both working in the yard on a day off. They might laugh while they watched Marky run under the sprinklers then. Or Terry might show them a chord change on the guitar she'd just learned. An overdue notice from Visa might come in and ruin the weekend for him. That would be the next tragedy—light and easy to take care of. It was horrible what Trey was thinking just then, and he wished his mind didn't dredge up the thought:

Thank God it wasn't us. Thank God my children weren't inside that house.

Along with this came the unspoken thought:

Just don't think about those other children, the older ones, Jenny and her friend, trapped by the Gorgon, with no escape but death.

CHAPTER 51

Five minutes later, in his glassed-in office, Oscar pushed a paper cup of coffee across the desk. "No cream, but you'll live. You want doughnuts, we got cream-filled and glazed, no plain." He slapped a pink box on a side table near his chair. He reached in and grabbed a crumbly half-doughnut and took a bite. Oscar spoke while he chewed. "I used to see things on a par with this back in my Hollywood days, but not since. Even then it wasn't nearly so bloody. My local boys, they've never seen this before. Half my guys were losing their lunches. I suppose, working with these kinds of killers, you've been somewhat exposed to this."

"A bit." Trey nodded. "But when it's on the inside of Darden State, it doesn't seem as terrible. Usually, they do it more to themselves than to others."

Trey stared at the coffee.

Then he picked up the cup and took a sip. It tasted sour. "She killed Jenny."

Oscar nodded his head, chewing the doughnut. "And a boy."

"I saw the body in the room. Who was it?"

"Jenny Reed's boyfriend, Tom Hyslop. They must've been surprised in the house. Jenny was in the kitchen. The boy was in the back bedroom." Oscar finished off his doughnut and reached into his breast pocket. He withdrew his pipe, thrusting it between his lips. "It's your wife with the asthma, am I right?"

Trey nodded. "Feel free to light up."

"Gracias." Oscar struck a match on the desk and cupped it in his hand around the pipe bowl.

"De nada," Trey replied, having learned a thing or two from his wife's family.

"You fool around with this Reed girl?" Oscar asked.

"Excuse me?"

"Jenny Reed. She was pretty. A pretty baby-sitter. Many men might think about it. Maybe fantasize. She probably had a crush on you, no?"

"What in God's name are you driving at?"

"Agnes Hatcher. Maybe she was jealous of this girl."

Trey would have laughed if he weren't so insulted. "I guess character is something that nobody respects in Southern California, but I've got some. I wouldn't cheat on my wife even if the opportunity arose."

"But if it did arise . . ."

"You don't know Agnes Hatcher either. She killed Jenny Reed because Jenny Reed was in the cottage. She would've killed Carly or Teresa or Mark if they'd been there."

"She didn't touch your children. I take that back, she didn't hurt your children. And you didn't mention yourself. What do you think Hatcher would've done had you been there?"

Trey thought a moment. His mind was a blank, short-circuited by the recent events. He said the first thing that came into his head. "I think she didn't want me to be there, knowing her. Once she figured out where I was staying, she could've waited until I arrived. She could've hidden somewhere. But she didn't. Unfortunately, she wanted to kill anyone else she came across."

"Just for the thrill?"

Trey shook his head, setting the half-empty cup back on the desk. "No. She does get a thrill from it, but not for the reasons generally associated with psychopaths. She believes she's collecting time in eternity for herself with each murder. She told me once that that was why the ancients sacrificed humans: to ransom their own souls. She had a whole theory about it."

"Why do you think she spared your son?"

Without hesitation Trey said, "He has my smell."

"Your smell?"

"Agnes Hatcher studies people. She studied me for years, even after she stopped seeing me. She knew more about me than anyone but my immediate family by then. She remembered smells. She remembered faces. She once told me that she could tell if a person had the heart of a killer or not. She could smell that too."

A grin rose from Oscar's doughnut-crumbled lips. "But you knew she was insane."

Trey shrugged. "No. The courts called her that. She felt she was a different species from the rest of us. She may have been right."

"Does she think *you* have the heart of the killer?"

Trey didn't answer this.

"In any case"—Oscar blew smoke from his pipe—"what she did to those teenagers was not just killing. It had the look of a ritual to it. We're not even sure that all the internal organs are there with either body . . ."

Trey wiped his face with his hand, remembering the skinned body in the bed. "God."

"I'm not going to go into detail about what was done to those kids. Suffice it to say, they didn't suffer long. And we caught her accomplice."

"She usually works alone."

Oscar nodded. "Or she kills whoever helps her. He's in the holding cell. He's a wild one. Named Nathaniel Coker, but known around the waterfront in San Pedro as Cobra. Not very bright. He was suspected of several murders of a group of Vietnamese fishermen several years back, but there was nothing solid to connect him to the crimes. The Hatcher woman tried to get him too. But she failed. It's good to know she fails now and then, huh? She didn't have the time, but she was going for his balls. She heard the girl screaming for help though, so she got out of there fast. Our friend Cobra only got gouged a bit, but we patched him up." Oscar winked. "Better than losing the ol' *cojones,* eh?"

"She's after me," Trey said after he finished the cup of coffee.

"I know," Oscar said. "She told your son that. She told him that she wanted his daddy. We found him standing on the patio, shivering. She had left a nice little lipstick mark on his forehead. Only it wasn't lipstick. It was blood. And it's all he would tell us. 'The lady wants my daddy.' You ask him, he'll probably tell you too. It's all he seems able to say at the moment."

For a second Trey felt defensive of his son. Not just with Agnes Hatcher, but even with the police. He didn't like the thought of Mark being questioned. Not after what he'd witnessed. He liked even less the idea of Mark being brought into court one day in the future to testify, while Agnes Hatcher sat there, watching the boy. *If* Agnes was ever caught. "Can't you get a helicopter for my family? I want them back on the coast as quickly as possible."

"We could do an airlift," Oscar said, relighting his pipe as if it would help him to think better. He tilted his head side to side, weighing this option. "I don't think it's necessary. Your son is strong. He'll come out of this soon. There's just something inside him that's keeping the door locked for a while. Until he feels absolutely safe." Oscar glanced at his watch. "We can have a helicopter here in thirty minutes, forty, tops. But you and your family can get on a boat in ten minutes and have two armed guards as an escort right now. If she's still around on this island, I think you should go for the boat. Why wait and chance anything?"

"I guess the boat's fine," Trey said. "But I'm staying."

"No you're not."

"If you want to catch Agnes Hatcher," Trey said. "You're going to need me. Once she knows I'm off this island, she's as good as slipped through your hands. I know her. I know what drives her."

"What drives her, then?" Oscar leaned forward. The smoke from his pipe blew right into Trey's eyes. Oscar apologized, fanning the air.

Trey took five minutes and told Oscar about the Jack the Ripper reincarnation story. "She operates on the part of the body where she thinks the soul resides for each person. She claims that Jack taught her that when she finds this sacred place of the soul, she gains another incarnation. That it's like a sacrifice to the fates. She thinks she's a different species. She believes I am too. She believes that she and I have to come together again to resolve, I don't know, some kind of karmic debt. We're bound through eternity. Not to be too morbid, but I assume she cut out Jenny's eyes."

Oscar leaned forward, pipe thrust firmly in mouth. "Why do you say that?"

"Jenny had beautiful eyes. They were her best feature. Agnes probably intuited that from just seeing her once. So she thought her soul resided in her eyes. I don't know this boy, Tom, but if he were in bed, waiting for Jenny, Agnes must've cut off his genitals."

"Right on the money," Oscar said, shaking his head. "With the Reed girl, it was more than just eyes." He thrummed his fingers on his desk. "I trained in L.A., Mr. Campbell, when I was younger. I've seen the worst a human being can do to another human being." He paused a beat. "This tops it. We know Hatcher took a quick shower to wash off the blood of her victims. We saw traces of her hair. It was red, and then, bits of it were blond. She used shampoo-in hair color. We also know she rummaged through your wife's closet. Probably changed clothes, although we didn't find Hatcher's clothes. She did this in just a few minutes. She's very fast as well as methodical. We assume, based on the time lag before we got the call for help from the neighbor, that she had about six minutes to get out of that house and avoid being seen by my men."

Trey covered his face with his hands. He remembered the kind of work that other killers in D Ward had done in the past. The images it brought up for him. Half of his job was repressing such memories. Carly was right; he was going to have to find another line of work. He didn't want his children to grow up in this atmosphere.

He didn't want to ever again see a look like the one on Mark's face that evening: the blank, empty gaze, the slight drool at the corner of his lips.

"Let's get your family on that boat," Oscar said, pushing himself up from his desk. He wiped his hand across the bald spot, swiping at several stray black hairs. "I've worked on this island for thirty years, Mr. Campbell. I never imagined anything like this monster would come here. What can I do to help catch her?"

Trey said the first thing that came into his mind. "Let me talk to the accomplice. Cobra."

CHAPTER 52

Carly dried her tears, but could not bring herself to let go of either of her children. She looked into Mark's eyes and tried speaking to him, but he stared through her. She remembered when he was born, how they'd called him Tadpole for months before the formal name Mark took hold. How he still seemed like her little Tadpole now, a baby, so sweet and loving. She wished she had brought the children with her and Trey for the afternoon. . . . If only she'd insisted on bringing them. They'd have been safer on a horse trail than in the cottage . . . *If only I'd been there* . . .

Teresa said, "I don't know why he couldn't run, Mommy." Her voice seemed now to be of a much younger girl, as if the experience she'd been through had taken away any maturity she'd developed. She began crying softly, and then stopped again. "I tried to make him run. Maybe I shoulda stayed with him." She nestled her head into her mother's shoulder.

"No, you did the right thing, Teresita," Carly whispered. "You got help, and if you hadn't've, maybe things would've been worse."

"He saw it all," Teresa said, gazing at her little brother. "I saw only the woman and the man and Jenny. I didn't see what they did to her. Marky saw it."

"It was a horrible thing," Carly said.

"Poor Jenny," Teresa said. "She's dead. If we'd been in the house, we'd be dead too . . ." She began crying. Carly felt the wetness of tears seep into her blouse. "Mommy, I want to go home."

"We will," her mother cooed. "We will. Soon." She glanced around the walls of the waiting area and felt as if Agnes Hatcher were there, waiting for them.

The woman who had stolen her children's innocence.

If only Trey had never worked at that damn hospital, she thought. None of this would have ever happened.

At that very moment Trey stepped back into the room.

CHAPTER 53

"They've got a police escort for you and the kids," Trey told his wife. He had to steel himself for this. His instinct was to go with them, to not let them out of his sight. He was afraid too. Afraid that Agnes Hatcher would get him, finally. That she would do to him what she did to others. He was having trouble even touching his wife. He was afraid that if he did, it would be too much like a good-bye.

He was afraid it would mean that they were returning to life.

And that he would never return to that mainland, not if Agnes Hatcher ever found him.

"You're not staying here," she said. "No. Not with that monster running loose." She jutted her jaw out a bit to emphasize her determination on this point.

"Carly, I have to," he said. "She's still here. I know her, Carly. I know what she wants."

Carly seemed like a fierce mother tiger defending her

young. An anger sparked into flame behind her eyes. He could see the heat in her face. "You told me she's a machine. If they don't catch her, she'll just kill you, Trey. And then I'll be a widow and your children will be fatherless. No. I can't let you do that. Not for some psycho or some job. Get your priorities straight."

"I have to stay," he said, defeated. "I can help catch her."

Carly said nothing. She still held Mark in her arms; he was wrapped in a cotton blanket. She took Teresa's hand. Teresa looked up at her father with tear-filled eyes. Her lower lip was trembling.

Trey wanted more than anything to go with them. But if he did, he might be leading Agnes Hatcher right to them.

He couldn't do that.

He had to trust his instincts on this.

Carly turned and left the police station. The whole way out, Teresa glanced back at her father, wide-eyed, as if wondering why he wasn't coming too.

There were no buildings to block the view to the harbor. The town was to the left, the sea straight ahead. Pelicans were gliding and diving near shore. The place possessed an unearthly silence. Jenny's family and the family of the dead boy would be notified. Residents and tourists would be staying in, and locking up tonight. Catalina Island would be run by fear until the Gorgon was caught.

Trey went and stood in the doorway. He wanted to go with Carly, but he was afraid that if he did, no one would ever catch Agnes Hatcher. Or, if he stayed with his family, maybe Agnes would turn up and kill all of them. He knew how to handle Hatcher. He knew how her mind worked. If he had only known that she was alive that day, he would never have left his family. He sent a mental prayer to Carly: *Turn around. Look at me again. Tell me you love me.*

She didn't turn back.

"Wait!" he called. He ran out, through the street, catching up with her.

When he did, he said, "I love you. I love you."

"I love you too," Carly said. Her eyes were dry. Her gaze was steady. The fire of anger was gone, replaced by resignation. "But do you love us enough to come with us? Do you love your children enough to stay with them?"

"That's not fair. If I can help in some way to catch her—"

Carly interrupted him. "I'm tired of watching our children get the worst part of you while the inmates of Darden State get the best part. We'll be in Long Beach tonight. When you're ready to, join us. We're your family."

Trey watched her walk with the children to a tall policeman. The policeman indicated one of the docks, where an L.A.P.D. boat was moored.

Trey watched them get on the motorboat—the tall policeman, and a short policewoman, who was the pilot.

He stayed and watched until the boat was under way.

He knew that once the police had caught Agnes Hatcher, Carly would understand and forgive him.

He knew he was doing the right thing.

From behind him, Oscar Arboles called out, "Mr. Campbell! Let's go see the snake in his pit."

CHAPTER 54

"Mommy?" Teresa asked as they got into the police motorboat.

"Sweetie?"

"Why isn't Daddy coming with us?"

"He has to help the police."

"Is that lady going to hurt Daddy?" Teresa asked.

"No," Carly said, not knowing if she might be lying to her own daughter.

CHAPTER 55

The holding cell of the Catalina police station was actually made up of two cells, side by side. They were each the size of small bathrooms. There was a toilet in each, and a sink. A narrow, short cot, alongside the toilet. No windows. The cell to the right, as Trey entered the area, was empty.

A man who looked like a young sailor turned middle-aged fast sat on the cot in the other cell.

He had blond hair, in a buzz cut to the sides, longish from there. He looked like a poster child for steroid abuses, because he had the bulky muscles and that strange, misformed kind of skull that seemed to accompany the use of such drugs.

His Hawaiian shirt was soaked with blood.

"Cobra, you have a visitor," Oscar said. He pointed to a chair for Trey to sit in. Then, to Trey, he said, "I'm going back to my computer to pull some things up. You need me, just yell. But yell loud."

CHAPTER 56

The cop on the boat was named Erskine. He had a longish face—like a hound dog, Carly thought. He was sweetly goofy, trying to make jokes with the policewoman who was piloting the boat. He flirted innocently enough with Carly, but she was in no mood for such nonsense. She felt numb inside, and the only heat within her was anger at Trey for not coming with them. Mark, wrapped in the blanket, was tucked against Teresa's arm.

"Excuse me," she said as the boat got under way. "How long will it take to get to Long Beach?"

Erskine smiled. "Well, the ocean's calm tonight, so it won't be bad. It might take as much as three hours. Four, if it gets choppy. You ever get seasick?"

"Sometimes," Carly said. She wrapped her arm around Teresa to help keep her warm.

The policewoman sitting in the pilot's chair was more businesslike. She kept her face forward and serenely guided the boat. Carly appreciated the fact that she hadn't tried to make small talk with them. She tried to watch the stars, but something of a fog was drifting in—the sky had been clear minutes before. This was what summer tended to be like near the coast. She hoped it wouldn't get any colder. The temperature could be seventy during the day, but then drop to a chilly sixty on the water at night. Carly closed her eyes, keeping her arm around her daughter and son.

Erskine made a few inane comments to the policewoman, which Carly couldn't hear. She was so furious with Trey for staying behind, the word *divorce* crossed her mind for a second. In her mind she smashed plates on the linoleum tile in their kitchen at home. In her mind she was the most loving and understanding wife possible. Neither extreme was true.

And then she thought: *He's doing the best he can. He's doing what he believes in.*

The other thought too:

Don't get hurt, Trey. Don't get hurt. Let the cops catch this woman, shoot her down, throw a net over her, whatever . . . don't get yourself in trouble.

Erskine said to the policewoman, "So, what's it like working on an island? Not a lot of action." He was from San Pedro, brought out three hours earlier, only to turn around again. He glanced at her badge. "Stouffer. Like the frozen dinners."

"Paula," she said, shooting him a nasty look. Erskine was taken aback for a second. She had seemed like a looker to him until he noticed her mean little eyes. They were almost squinty, and he always thought women were somehow tainted if they had squinty little eyes. Then the look vanished from her face. Her eyes widened, doelike. She was a babe again. "What's it like on the mainland?" she asked.

"Oh, I don't know. I don't do much work in the harbor or anything. Mainly burglaries. Stolen cars. The usual."

The policewoman said nothing.

"I'm sure I saw you at the academy," Erskine said. "I never forget a face."

Paula Stouffer half smiled. "I've lectured at various academies."

"On what? Island hopping?" He was trying to make a joke, but it died in his mouth. He knew how feeble it sounded. "That killer back there was some doozy. Did you see the blood on the walls?"

Paula Stouffer nodded. "Listen, can you steer for a minute? I want to get a smoke from my bag."

Erskine nodded. "Sure. I love piloting these babies." He kept his eyes straight forward. It was pitch black, the sun having set just a brief while earlier, but there was always an incipient light along the horizon where the mainland began.

He felt the policewoman's hand on his shoulder, and he grinned, feeling like maybe he was going to get lucky tonight.

Her grip on his shoulder got stronger, sharper.

Carly's head drooped to the side until it was completely leaning on Teresa's. Teresa had fallen asleep too.

Only Mark was awake.

Only Mark, wrapped in the blanket with his eyes wide, saw what happened to the policeman named Erskine. The dim green lights from the edges of the boat cast a shadow as the knife plunged into Erskine's neck. The policewoman cut so sharply into Erskine's throat that his head fell almost completely backward.

When the policewoman finished, she turned a key in the boat's ignition. She stepped around her seat. She walked calmly over and leaned close to Mark.

She had handcuffs in one hand.

In the other, a fishing knife.

Mark saw her shadow face.

Mark gasped, "The lady."

CHAPTER 57

In the holding cell area of the Catalina police station, Trey Campbell sat down in the folding chair. The place was gray and made of concrete. The bars were thick. Cobra had been finger-painting on the gray wall of his cell with his own feces. He'd painted a snake, complete with forked tongue.

And he'd painted a woman. Stick figure. Oval breasts. A halo around her head.

Cobra glanced over at him. Saw that he noticed his recent art. Seemed proud of it. He seemed so different than other human beings would be in the same situation. This man seemed as if he owned the world in which he existed.

Trey knew then. He could feel it the way he felt it about the psychos on his ward. The way he knew about the doorman when he'd been a little kid. Cobra was one of them. Trey felt that chill, and the slight confusion. The sense that there was something so different about Cobra that it verged on paranoia. Or a complete understanding at the subliminal level of another human being. Cobra was of the same species as Agnes—but not as smart.

"I like to draw," Cobra said.

"Did you draw the word 'beloved' on the wall at that cottage?"

Cobra shook his head. "That's a word. I don't do words. I draw pictures. You like?" He tapped the wall with the snake. "It's me and her. She's righteous. She's . . ." He seemed to burst with possible descriptions of her. Then he said, "She's everything."

"Tell me about her," Trey said. Faking calm, he placed his hands carefully on his knees and didn't look Cobra directly in the eye, but just past his left ear. He didn't want to get into mind games with this guy.

Cobra grinned. He had a wide gap between his front teeth. When he spoke, his voice was gravelly. "She's a goddess. She touched the face of the universe, man." Then, leaning forward, "You got a cigarette?"

Trey shook his head. "I don't smoke. Sorry."

As if this were enough grounds for dismissal, Cobra leaned back on the cot. He crossed his arms behind his head and shut his eyes.

"Tell me about her."

"Why should I? You can't even get me a cigarette. You some lowlife ragpicker trying to get me to confess? You can sit on it and rotate."

Trey got up and walked out of the cell. As he did, Cobra called out, "I like Marlboro Lights 100 in a box!"

In the hall he found a cigarette machine. He borrowed change from Oscar and got the pack that Cobra wanted.

Trey brought the cigarettes into the holding cell area. He passed a cigarette and a book of matches in to Cobra.

Cobra took them, touching Trey's slightly trembling hand.

"Don't be scared of me," Cobra said. "I'm only the tool. She's the operator, let me tell you. I could've sat out my days at the docks stealing from the till here and there. Nothing like this . . ." He lit the cigarette and inhaled deeply. "This . . . magnificence . . . this brilliance."

"You mean Agnes?"

Cobra nodded. "Thank you for the cigarette. You are truly a compassionate man." He said this with mock refinement.

"Do you know where she is?"

Cobra grinned. He had a grin like a sideshow barker: sleazy and compelling at the same time. "You're the one, ain't you?"

Trey said nothing.

Cobra laughed. "You're the one she's looking for. Those kids we took out. They wasn't. They was fun for her. She told me she was collecting lifetimes to give you. On a platter, buddy."

"What do you mean?" Trey sat down in the chair by the cell. He leaned forward.

"Before I say anything, can you get me a good lawyer?"

"What?"

"I'm an accomplice to murder. I know that. I'll be happy to turn evidence against her, but only if I got me a good lawyer. One who's gonna make sure she never gets out again. I know her now. It only took me a day, but I know her inside and out. She's that way. Can you pass me that pack?" he asked, his hand out in supplication. "I like to chain-smoke."

Trey passed the cigarette pack to Cobra. Again Cobra's hand grazed the underside of his palm.

Cobra quickly lit one cigarette off the first. He stubbed out the last of the first cigarette and began smoking the next. The room was filling with smoke.

"I can't do much with regards to lawyers," Trey said.

"Oh." Cobra puffed on the cigarette. "I guess I got nothing to say to you, in that case."

He swiveled around on the cot and lay down.

"She's going to get you anyway," Trey said, standing from the chair. He walked toward the door.

As he touched the doorknob, Cobra made a sputtering cough. "What?" he cried out. "Whatju say?"

Trey turned, leaning back against the door. "She's going to get you. Because you know her. She gets everyone who sees her in action. When she was caught last time, she had entire file cabinets with descriptions of people who knew about her, and their families, and anyone who had ever come in contact with them. She was going to systematically operate on each of them. Even if it took several lifetimes. I may not be able to get you a lawyer, Cobra, but I can be a pretty decent witness. I know her. I know that she's the one who went for the girl's eyes and face. And I know why. I know that it was her, not you, who cut off the boy's penis and killed him. You were just the—what would you call it?—the tough guy who scared those kids. You played with them after they were dead. You were the one who didn't know how far she'd go."

"Shit," he said, his voice raspy with smoke. "I didn't even know she was gonna kill 'em. I thought we was just gonna rough 'em up and have some fun with 'em. I like blood and all, but not the way she did."

"So," Trey said. "Where is she?"

Cobra cursed and kicked the toilet. "She really screwed me."

"Yeah, she did. Royally."

When the man in the cell had calmed down some, he said, "I thought we was just gonna, you know, have fun and scare those kids. She told me she was after you 'cause of that whole past-lifetime bullshit. I held that boy . . ." Cobra began bawling like a baby. While he cried, he still managed to smoke. Trey knew the tears were fake. Cobra was a sociopath. Cobra couldn't even understand that what he had just participated in, the murders of Jenny and her boyfriend, was wrong. He would think the mistake was in getting caught. If his tears were at all real, it was because he was caught, not because of remorse.

Trey went back to the folding chair and sat down. "Where is Agnes Hatcher?"

Cobra wiped his eyes, shuddering with tears. He took a long drag off a fresh cigarette. "Do you know about time and space? I mean, how she thinks about it? She sounds like friggin' Einstein, you ask me. She talks about some kind of continuing thing . . ."

"A time and space continuum," Trey said.

"Yeah. You do know her. The intersection, she said, of time and space. She collected all these things, you know, bits of hearts and lungs and livers, I thought she was some kind of cannibal, but she didn't want to eat them. She told me they were for the path. The crossroads of time and space. They were the fuel to the path. She talked like she'd been there. Like she knew where she was going. It was wild." He said this as if it were some wonderful trip. "You want to know where she is?" he asked rhetorically. "I mean, you're never gonna find her. I tried to tell the other cops, but they weren't like you . . . they were morons. You want me to tell you? I can tell you, but you won't get it unless you know her. Unless you know her real well. She told me only one man was gonna understand it. Where she was going."

He snorted and laughed, a big hyena laugh. "You're the one, ain't you? You're the love of her life, I can tell. She told me all about you. What you did before. Seems like you should be inside here and me out there. How many women, mister? Ten, twelve? Slicing and dicing. Doin' things to them that no man oughta do. But you wanna know something? She let me do her, mister. She put out for me."

Trey listen dispassionately. "I understand she attacked you too."

Instinctively, Cobra clutched his crotch.

Trey said, "It's because of what she let you do to her. If she remains free, Cobra, she's going to finish that job. I know her. She's a machine. She never starts something without finishing it. So tell me where she is."

Cobra, looking frightened for the first time in the cell, told everything he knew.

CHAPTER 58

On the boat at sea, Carly opened her eyes when she heard her son speak.

"The lady," Mark said over and over.

Carly looked up at the policewoman. Carly kissed Mark on the forehead. *He's getting better. He'll be fine. This nightmare will be over soon.* "That's right, Marky. The police lady." The mist of fog, like a thin veil, drifted across the boat.

"The lady," Mark said again. Carly was about to say something to the policewoman, to ask why the boat had stopped, when she saw the large knife in the woman's hands.

The kind of knife that she herself had used a few times to help Trey gut and clean the fish they'd caught.

The policewoman held it against Mark's throat.

"You're Agnes Hatcher," Carly gasped. She didn't

want to move for fear of what this madwoman would do to her son.

"And you're the bitch who stole my Jack from me," Agnes Hatcher said. "I can smell him all over you."

CHAPTER 59

Trey felt like he was moving through molasses, from the holding cell area to the door. He heard Cobra's cynical laughter and tasted the smoke in the air. He pushed through the door to the corridor that led to the offices of the police station. He passed a middle-aged man sitting at a desk, scribbling notes down from a phone call. He walked swiftly to Oscar's office, knocking on the door.

Through the glass Oscar glanced up from his computer. He signaled for Trey to enter.

Trey opened the door and said triumphantly, "I know where she is. She's at the caves. It's because of the connection to the word *Whitechapel.* It's a sign to her of where time and space will intersect. Where our karma will be resolved."

"Capilla Blanca," Oscar said without hesitation. "Maybe that's it. Glad our Cobra talked to somebody.

None of my boys could get through to him. Anything else?"

"He said she's keeping souvenirs."

"Body parts? Organs?"

Trey nodded.

It was nine P.M.

CHAPTER 60

"You stay here," Oscar said, rising, grabbing his jacket from the coatrack. "Watch TV or talk to Dinah out front. I'll get ten men and some motorboats over there. We'd go up to the other end of the cliffs, but I already have men out on the road setting up blocks. I doubt she'd've had time to go that way. For all I know, she knows her way around in a boat. And if she's there, I don't want her finding you. How'd you get our friend in the cell to tell you this?"

"I've worked with sociopaths for years," Trey said. "I understood him."

Oscar lip-farted at this, as if Trey were just some bleeding heart.

"You'll never find her without me," Trey said.

Oscar turned and pointed at him. "You think too much of yourself. You need some rest. There's a couch out front. Use it."

Trey felt stunned by the authoritative command from him.

Several minutes later he went to sit on the green couch in the front office. Dinah, the dispatch officer, listened to the police band, which she kept on low volume. She smiled occasionally when Trey looked her way, but kept her head down.

He watched the silent television. There was no news about the murders. He wondered how sensational a murder had to be to make the news.

He closed his eyes. He wished he'd gone with Carly. He wasn't needed here. Whether or not Agnes Hatcher was after him, he didn't need to be there for her. He should be there for his family.

He imagined Carly playing with Mark out at the swimming pool. Teresa, diving off the far edge.

Mark afraid of his own reflection, which lurked at the bottom of the pool.

Without wanting to, Trey Campbell fell asleep.

He dreamed.

A chess game in hell, between him and Agnes Hatcher. All around them, fire.

She was picking her queen up and moving it toward his knight.

"You can't win like that," he said.

Agnes Hatcher grinned. Her teeth were bloodstained. "I don't have a strategy," she said. "Do you, Mr. Campbell? Mr. Campbell?" she asked, her voice melting into another voice, lighter, sweeter. . . .

Trey awoke when he heard his name being called.

It was Dinah. "Mr. Campbell?"

His eyes fluttered open. He oriented himself to the room. The front office of the Catalina police station. He sat up. His back was all sweaty from lying against the leather couch. He wiped at his neck.

"Mr. Campbell?" Dinah repeated. She stood up from behind her desk.

He nodded. "Uh-huh."

Dinah turned up the dispatch radio a bit, but it sounded like several voices speaking in monotones all at once. She turned it down again. "Oscar wants me to tell you they've caught her."

Trey glanced up at the clock on the wall.

It was almost ten P.M.

CHAPTER 61

A half hour later, when Oscar stepped into the police station, he was soaked to the skin. "The damn waves," he said, "I was either throwing up or getting soaked. We could barely see anything because the fog's coming in. I was sure we were going to crash into each other."

Trey had been pacing for almost a half hour. "So what's the story?"

Oscar glanced at him like he was the last person in the world he wanted to see. "The story is just about the way I'd've played it. We went out to those caves. My men and women are already coming down with colds, and the ones out of San Pedro think I'm a joke. We spend an hour and a half shining flashlights up and down the slimy walls of that Capilla Blanca. Although I must admit, that central room, the round one with the well in the middle, is pretty interesting. I've lived here for fifteen years and never went through there. It's amazing how those monks lived. . . ." Realizing he was getting off the subject, he backtracked. "So we spend half the night looking there, and I get this call. Not on the general police band, but on my private band. Turns out the coast guard picked up a woman matching Hatcher's description, soaked in blood, on a sloop just up out to sea a bit. She was easy to subdue, and they're taking her to the mainland. So, we're all a little furious we ran off on a tip from a paranoiac. And I don't mean our friend Cobra." Oscar sneezed, and walked past Trey.

Trey stood there in the center of the office.

"I don't believe it," he said.

Oscar stopped at the door to his own office. He shook his head. "Believe it, Campbell. All I can say is, I hope they fry that woman. She deserves worse, but if there's a hell, she'll work out her damn karma from there."

"It's not her, Oscar," Trey said. "I know it."

"And how do you know that?"

"Instinct," Trey said.

Defeated, Trey walked out the door, out of the police station, into the cool night. He passed the closed-up storefronts where Carly had window-shopped earlier that same evening. The ice cream stand, where he'd been sitting, thinking how good life could be. *It can all turn on a dime.* He remembered a biblical quote: *In the twinkling of an eye.* He wished he could step back through time, to that moment in the morning when he had forbidden Mark from coming horseback riding. If he'd followed through on Carly's plan, even Jenny and her boyfriend would still be alive, because the cottage would've been empty. Then he might've been able to prevent those murders. And he would've prevented his son and daughter from having been exposed to that . . .

creature. The thought gave him shivers: Agnes Hatcher kissing her son on his forehead. Like an animal cleaning another before the kill.

The Gorgon was in his life again. For all the good he tried to do her, none of it mattered. He had tried to understand her pathology when she'd been first admitted to Darden. He had been young and idealistic and, essentially, stupid. He had given her information that fueled her fantasies.

Trey could not have felt worse.

He walked down the street to the docks. When he reached the pier, he sat down and gazed out at the night. The fog was light, and he could see the darkness of the sea. He closed his eyes, sending a prayer out for Mark to get better.

And then, with sudden clarity, he remembered something that Agnes Hatcher had once told him.

He'd been sitting with her, playing chess. She was a much better chess player than he'd ever be. It was in the recreation room at Darden State. Orderlies were standing guard at the doors. Agnes was rarely allowed around any other patients.

She wore the hospital gown and green slippers. Her hair sparkled in the sunlight that cut through the barred windows.

He leaned back in the chair. It was his move, but he couldn't figure out for the life of him how to get around her queen.

She said, "It's a strategy."

He grinned, back then. He was only twenty-three, and he still believed that people could be saved from themselves. From their past, their psyches. "What is?"

"This." She indicated the plastic chess pieces. "It's my strategy. You don't have one. You're just reacting to mine. That's not how anyone wins."

"How can I win? You're going to put me in check soon. You always do."

She looked quite seriously at him. "I would never do anything to hurt you. I don't want you to lose this game." She said it then as if what she were saying was of some great importance. "I want you to win."

"Why?"

"Because you understand."

"About chess?"

"About how all of it is one. Chess, life, death . . . You're not like the others. You have special knowledge. Only you need to open the door to it. You need the key. I am the key."

He let this go. He knew that she was insane. There were some things the patients said that were indecipherable.

Then she said, "Remember this. I always have a strategy. In this game, have you watched? I moved my men around to this side, and so you followed. And then to the other side, and then you followed again. And back and forth. But if you watch the pattern of what I did, you'll see a thread through the middle. This is where I moved my queen. This was no strategy at all."

"Right where you started. All your other moves were distractions from that main move." He nodded. "I wished I had noticed it. That's some strategy: I'm dumb and you're smart."

"No," she said, leaning across the board to touch his hand. "My strategy is making you see that there is no strategy. All of it is chance. Fate. Fate is the guiding star. I believe fate guides us to where we need to go. I may appear to win this game, and you may appear to lose it. . . ." The warmth of her hand grew stronger until he wanted to draw back from it. It was too warm. Too inviting. "But fate is what draws my queen to her destination. The men may go to the left to fight, and to the right, but the players move where they are meant to, regardless. Your castle is mine, your kingdom, because it was meant to be mine."

With that, she moved her queen and won the game.

He opened his eyes. The bay at Avalon was before him. He stood up on the pier. He tried to look out to the bend of the island, but could not see any of the Kirk in the Rocks.

The men may go to the left to fight and to the right.
But the players move where they are meant to.
My strategy is no strategy.
Fate is the guiding star.
Your castle is mine.
Your kingdom.

CHAPTER 62

Agnes Hatcher knelt in darkness on the deck of the boat. She waited until the last patrol boat had rounded the curve of the island. She had used the boat's police radio, and, from her years lecturing to police academies, she knew which band to use to make the frequency appear distant enough to fool the local police. She had spent most of her childhood and youth observing and studying the police. It always came in handy.

She was less exhausted than exhilarated from the day's kill. Operating on the boy and girl at the cottage had been refreshing, and she had showered in the spray from the teenage girl. When she heard the other girl, the little one, go running and screaming, she knew she had to get out of the cottage fast. She did not intend to be caught before she attained fulfillment.

She would've taken his son, then.

The beautiful boy, so much like his father's smell.

But there had been no time that afternoon.

Instead, she had gone back inside the cottage, pulled some clothes from the woman's closet, and changed into them. They were long for her, the shorts and T-shirt, but she had no time to worry about such things. She wrapped her jeans and sweater in a bundle with the soul catchers. Then she went out the front door of the cottage, leaving Cobra shivering in a corner of the kitchen, spineless man that he was.

Since the little girl was screaming at the road behind the cottage, no one seemed to notice the woman in shorts and T-shirt jogging down the side path, as if she were just out for exercise.

The police bitch was easy to take care of. She was down at the docks, totally inexperienced, young too—perhaps only twenty-one.

She was alone, because all the other cops had gone up to the cottage. Except Paula Stouffer had not wanted to. She'd been scared. She'd never done more, probably, than catch a teenager shoplifting. She might have even known the girl and boy who had been slaughtered up the hill.

It was easy to approach her as a tourist and tell her that there was someone funny in the rest rooms at the pier. Someone funny, not too scary. Just a weirdo.

"I'll go with you," Agnes had said. "I just think there's something wrong with the poor man."

Paula Stouffer was undoubtedly relieved that she didn't have to deal with murder and mayhem. Only someone funny, perhaps a homeless person, in the women's rest room.

When Agnes had her inside the filthy walls, she ripped the knife across Paula Stouffer's throat, using her own sweater to sop up the blood so that it didn't ruin the police uniform.

She stuffed the body into the last stall. Covered her

with one of the dark plastic bags that was used to line the rest room garbage can. She closed the stall door, locking it from the inside. Then she climbed over the top of the stall.

But only after she scalped her, for Paula had beautiful auburn hair.

It had been that simple. She knew that there would be a boat to the mainland with his family on board. She'd been hoping he would come too. But it was enough that she had his family.

Their lives, their sacrifice, would be more crucial toward immortality than any others.

There was no moon that night. The fog came and went as if an unfelt wind moved it along. The boat was dark too, for she'd shut off all the controls.

But even so, against the stars and mist and indigo sky she saw the great Church of Fate rising, triumphant.

She glanced at the silhouettes of her prisoners:

The woman handcuffed to the girl, and the boy. The woman was gagged, and Agnes had draped a piece of cloth, torn from Officer Erskine's shirt, over her face. The bitch would feel what Agnes had felt all those years. The bitch would know what Agnes had been through.

And the boy. So like his father. He would not try to escape. She knew that.

She held tight to the fishing knife. It was so much like the knife they had used together in the fall of 1888. The taste of the blood that day had reminded her of all the lives they'd captured then.

Of all the lifetimes they had acquired.

He would come to her now.

He would come.

CHAPTER

63

Trey didn't bother knocking at Oscar Arboles's office. He just walked in.

"She *is* there," Trey said.

Oscar glanced up. "Mr. Campbell." He didn't seem as furious as Trey had expected him to be.

The police chief looked sad, his eyes bloodshot.

"We were wrong," Oscar said. "There was no coast guard pickup. I located the frequency of the call—the one that claimed that Agnes Hatcher had been caught. I'm afraid I have some bad news for you."

Trey stood still.

"Your family hasn't been sighted near the mainland. They should've been close to docking by now." Oscar said, "She somehow managed to take the boat. Overcome the officers. We found one of them, dead, scalped. Paula Stouffer. In the beach rest room, in a locked stall, covered with a garbage bag. Hatcher's been out to sea almost four hours. She destroyed any equipment on board, so we can't track her. She has your family."

Trey Campbell said, "I know. That was her goal all along. Checkmate."

Oscar looked at him, perplexed.

"She's at Capilla Blanca."

"No," Oscar said. "We went over every inch of that place. I'm sorry. She's probably on the mainland by now, or near it. Maybe she's hiding up at San José Island. Maybe she's on the western side of our own island. We have helicopters coming from Los Angeles to check the local harbors. No more goose chases. I'm sorry. It's out of my jurisdiction now. The state boys will have her shortly, I'm sure."

But Oscar said this as if even he did not believe it.

CHAPTER 64

Trey ran down the streets of Avalon, his mind racing ahead of him. He had no one to turn to now. He was going to get no help from the police. They had their own agenda, their own strategy when it came to catching killers like Agnes. It often took days to track down such killers. By then she might have added three more victims to her list. Usually, police were not that effective in the short term, for they didn't understand the nature of the beast they were hunting. Trey felt a cold sweat break out along his scalp and neck. He had to do something.

Time was running out. His family may already have been killed. But that wasn't what Agnes Hatcher would use them for. She would use them for drawing him to her.

He was not going to let anything happen to his wife and children.

He was not going to let them die at the hands of the monster.

He had only himself as a weapon.

But it was his best weapon, because Agnes Hatcher wanted him.

CHAPTER 65

"Out" was all Agnes said. She had the boy handcuffed to her left wrist. She motioned with the fishing knife toward the small beach of pebbles at the sea entrance to Capilla Blanca. The waves crashed just beyond the larger boulders, but she'd been able to maneuver around them because the police boat was just small enough. But if they stayed in the boat much longer, a wave was likely to come over the rocks and do more than just spray them.

"I said, out." Agnes took the knife and held it against the boy's neck.

The little girl, handcuffed to the woman, moved. Agnes could tell she was afraid of stepping out of the rocking boat. The girl's mother, her face covered, her mouth gagged, made no sound whatsoever.

The girl gingerly stepped down into the ankle-deep water, shivering. Her mother followed; the girl helped guide her over the edge of the boat. The mother almost fell, but balanced herself against the girl.

The boy at Agnes's side said nothing, but when she walked, he stayed with her.

Agnes grabbed two of the flares. She popped one of them, and a fizzing red flame struck at its tip. She handed this to the girl. "Use this like a candle," she said. "If you try anything, I will kill your brother right in front of you. If you run off any path with your mother handcuffed to you, keep in mind, there are pits and chasms throughout these caves. You and your mother will both die if you don't follow me exactly. Do you understand?"

The little girl nodded slowly, tears in her eyes.

Agnes lit her flare also, and held it in the hand that was cuffed to the boy. She said to him, "You will do exactly what I say, won't you?"

The boy looked up at her, staring blankly. He nodded.

"You saw what happened to your baby-sitter?"

Again Mark nodded. He was not even shivering. It was as if he had adapted to this situation. As if some mechanism within his unconscious mind had kicked in, shunting fear aside for the time being. As if survival at any cost were enough to keep him functioning.

"She was very bad. She was vain. That means she thought the beauty of her face was more important than the gods. But I took that face from her. I bit it with my teeth." Agnes leaned closer to Mark's face. "I tasted her face. It was where she lived. Do you know where you live?"

Mark said nothing, but he didn't take his eyes off her.

"You live in your heart, little boy. And that's where I'll go if I need to find you." She stood up again. The girl's face was red in the glow from the flare. "Be careful," Agnes said patiently. "Keep it away from your face. You might burn yourself."

She directed her captives to the cave's entrance.

CHAPTER 66

The Bayrunner Westcoaster was docked at the short pier. Trey Campbell had to climb over a low chicken-wire fence to get to it; the rental boat dock was closed after dark, unless one had a key. He squatted down beside it, stepping, crablike, into its stern. He slid across to one of the seats. He checked the motor for gas—there was still plenty. It took him several minutes to get it started, and when he did, he stayed down low in the boat in case one of the local cops was still out, watching the docks. He loosed the boat from its mooring.

He drove the boat around the docks, going slowly so as not to bump any of the other resting boats. He steered it out into the bay, watching the shore to see if anyone followed him. The worst thing now would be if Oscar and his team of police followed him. Agnes would surely murder his family in that event. Only Trey knew that he held the key to stopping her.

The sea was calm.

Once he was out far enough from the town of Avalon, with its flickering lights, he noticed an incipient light across the sea, a greenish glow, as the waves crashed against rock and shoreline. He knew to keep the boat a good distance from the shore, because although part of the island was smooth with sand, there were outlaw rocks at sandbars just out in the bay, creating a fake reef. When the boat rounded the side of the island to where Capilla Blanca rose up, he turned the motor off.

It was a silent night.

The night mist moved silently.

Trey took the oars beneath the slats of the boat and began slowly rowing toward the cavern's mouth.

Agnes Hatcher's words echoed in his mind:

My strategy is no strategy.

Then he thought: *She thinks I'm Jack the Ripper. She believes we have to make things right together. That's what she's after. Not Mark or Terry or Carly. They're just in the way.*

She has no strategy. It's more haphazard than planned. Even her escape, it was pure dumb luck. It was Donna Howe being foolish and Rob Fallon being his ever-lovin' sociopathic self. It wasn't fate. These were random events, which she has made to look like part of a pattern. I was caught up in it because I was afraid. I wasn't seeing it for what it was: the machine called the Gorgon just going where the wind took her, the easiest roads, the dumb luck of life. Her finding my vacation phone and address was coincidental to attacking Donna Howe. If Jim Anderson hadn't passed that piece of paper to Donna, Agnes would probably be at his residence in Redlands. Not here. It's all chance, and she's relying on it while the cops are looking for logic and pattern.

But her logic is nightmares.

The answer to stopping her is within her own pathology.

Becoming a nightmare.

Becoming what she wants.

An idea that seemed absurd and brilliant at the same time suddenly occurred to him, something he'd never really considered. Something about telling Mark his as-if philosophy.

Trey Campbell was going to behave as if Agnes Hatcher's pathology were real.

He was going to become, for her, Jack the Ripper.

He was going to give her what she wanted.

He only hoped he wasn't too late for his family.

Rowing as fast as his heart and muscles would bear, he saw what he thought was the flash of a red flare just up at the shore, in the mouth of the cavern.

CHAPTER 67

The flare lit the cave a brilliant red, outlining its recesses and sharply jutting rocks. Teresa walked carefully along the wet pebbles at the cave bottom. As she was about to step on what seemed a smoother surface, the psycho woman shouted at her, "Not that way!" Then, more calmly, "To the left, dear. See how it winds upward. If you go straight ahead, we'll wind up in a lagoon. Look, do you see the spiral of the path? It represents the journey home. Spiraling, spiraling."

Teresa looked up at her mother's face. It was covered, but she could tell by the way her mother was walking that she wanted Teresa to obey the orders. Not seeing her mother's face was kind of scary for her; the handcuffs that bound them together hurt her wrists too. But she knew her father would come, with the police, soon. She knew it would work out okay, just like it did on television shows like *Rescue 911*. Teresa had an opposing thought in her head too. She thought that what happened to Jenny might happen to her. She tried not to let that thought control her.

Teresa went to the left. She kept the flare as far out in front of her as possible. It was warm at its base. Too warm, as far as she was concerned. She didn't like the way the fire sputtered at its tip either. It wasn't like a Fourth of July sparkler. It felt too warm, like it was going to eventually get so hot that she'd have to drop it. She didn't want to be in the dark with the psycho woman.

She glanced back at Mark, cuffed to the woman.

Mark looked like he was somewhere else. His feet moved, and he stepped over rocks. But he didn't seem to be normal in his eyes.

Teresa stepped up onto a rough, narrow path that quickly rose up from the wet pebbles. Before her she saw the path rise and twist, like a staircase in a lighthouse. She hoped there were no wild animals living in it.

She didn't want to turn around and see the woman behind her. She didn't want to ever have to look at that face again.

She hoped everything would turn out all right.

Teresa tugged at the handcuff to keep her mother away from the edge of the path.

CHAPTER 68

Agnes gave her own flare to the boy. She whispered, "You hold on to this. It'll help us see. You can chase away all the shadows with it." She showed him how to hold it. He was a beautiful boy. Just like his father. She wanted to hug him tight because he had a spark of her lover in him. But she knew this wasn't the time.

Then, as she followed the girl and her mother up the winding path, she opened the police knapsack at her side. Remembering when she first spoke with Jack in this new incarnation, the walks through the garden, the chess games, the way she looked at him and knew . . .

Agnes Hatcher left a trail for him. Each of the pieces was sacred, and he would follow them to their nest.

He would follow them, and remember.

* * *

The lightning flashed in her brain, and she saw:

The oven was stuffed with rage. The oil jug, for the lamps upstairs, rested in the corner. The coppers had left after searching the place. They had run back to the dead woman in the street. The one with her body sliced open. The one whose blood tasted like warm metal.

The locket was in her hands, open.

The lock of hair.

The picture.

She looked at the oil lamp. She could hear the whistles outside, and the endless rain. Would it never stop? She went to the casement window, looking through the grate. The street was enshrouded with fog. The rain was not as heavy as it sounded against the room. It sounded like drums beating; but it was only spitting rain outside.

She took the locket in her fist and crushed it, but it would not break. It only seemed to get warmer with her touch.

The time was drawing near. She knew that she must act fast, or she would never have the chance. How could he betray her?

A memory of being told a story as a little girl: of a witch pushed into a great oven and baked alive by merry children.

Agnes stepped over to the oil lamp, lifting it up. Its glow was warm. Warmth enveloped her suddenly. The locket in her hand was like fire. The lamp's glow, so comforting.

In the corner, the great oven.

Lightning thrust its spear through her—

She was in the motel in Las Cruces. He was peeling away the layers of her face. He was showing her that she wore a mask.

"Do you see who you are?" he asked. "It takes several lifetimes for ordinary people to understand this. But I'm giving you a gift of sight. You see? Remember the past? Your life was different then, but it was your true self."

Red lightning cut across her vision like blood blinding her from her cut forehead—

She was in the cave, and the boy handcuffed to her stared up at her with the eyes of one who knows.

CHAPTER 69

Trey was up to his shoulders in the water, drawing his boat toward the shore. He had to stop the motor several yards from the ragged beach because the waves were getting slightly choppy. He was not a good enough seaman to ensure that he wouldn't crash the rented boat on the rocks. He gradually found sure footing, and was able to bring the boat up to the narrow strip of beach, just beyond the rocks. He secured it as best he could, and then went over to the police transport boat. He found Erskine's body, and a pool of blood in an aura around his neck and shoulders.

Without hesitation he reached into the dead man's shoulder holster and withdrew a gun. It was a standard issue Smith & Wesson. From Trey's limited knowledge of cops, he assumed that the dead officer had rarely if ever used the gun. But it would be fully loaded.

Trey held it in his right hand. The idea of having to

shoot it bothered him. Conflicting images rose in his mind:

Shooting the old man who had been trying to break in to his house.

Agnes Hatcher, bent over the psychiatrist at Darden, bits of his scalp between her teeth.

He checked around the boat and found a small flashlight. He flicked it on. The police radio was destroyed. His first impulse was to take this boat, go get the police, and come back. But what if there was no time? What if there were only minutes left to help his children?

I can't risk it. I can't sacrifice them to that madwoman.

From within the cavern he saw a spray of red light. It moved, casting enormous shadows across the hanging rocks.

He waded through the tidal pool that would, within the next several minutes, be flooded.

When he stepped over the smaller rocks and across what seemed a lagoon within the cavern, he waved the flashlight beam about the cave.

Then he saw something that made him catch his breath.

He shined the light on the object that lay upon the slick path that led up from the water.

It was a human heart.

Beside it, one of Carly's sandals.

Trey Campbell felt a sudden sharp pain in the back of his head, and for a moment he thought he was falling.

Instead, he was leaning across a woman's body. Blood trickled from the edge of her neck. He looked up, and Agnes Hatcher was there—she looked different, but he knew her through the eyes. "The windows of the soul," she said.

He reached for her, and grasping her, brought her to him. Kissing her.

Trey opened his eyes. He was standing on the path that led to the Monk's Chamber. He felt dislocated, as if he'd briefly shared a vision with the Gorgon. *She's inside me now. I will find you, Agnes. I will keep you from hurting them.*

As he hiked the path that spiraled upward, he came across other such finds. What might've been an eye, although it was all bloody. Several yards ahead on the path, a ragged patch of human skin, almost like sheer fabric. *Don't let this be my children. Don't let this be Carly. Please, be safe. Please, Agnes, don't hurt them.* He wondered if he was too late. He moved as quickly as he could across the slick rock.

He shined his flashlight up the trail.

He knew where it led.

His father had taken him there many times when he'd been a boy.

The Monk's Chamber. The Monk's Well.

Capilla Blanca.

Whitechapel.

Trey shouted, "Agnes!"

The name echoed through the caverns, which to Trey now seemed like the spiraling chambers of a nautilus, all leading to the central place of destiny.

CHAPTER 70

The room was circular, with natural stone benches within its perimeter. A chasm was at its center, almost perfectly round, like a well without walls. However, there were several embedded rocks around its edges. The walls of the room were etched and shaded with pictures of Jesus and Mary. This made Teresa feel a little less scared. Graffiti, too, was sprayed and slashed across the white walls. Teresa began saying her prayers silently. She gripped her mother's hand.

Her mother gripped back, giving her a squeeze.

It felt like a signal from her mother that they would be safe.

Someone was yelling from below, almost like it was coming from the well that sat in the center of the room.

"Do you hear him?" Agnes said, turning to the children. The flares lit the room with a pink glow, and the psycho woman seemed to be bathed in blood on her face. She had eyes like fire.

The scream again, "Agnes!"

Teresa recognized the voice. *Daddy.* She glanced at Mark, but he still stared straight ahead, through her.

Agnes Hatcher grinned with bloodstained teeth. "It's the intersection," she said. "It's the sacrifice time."

She grabbed Mark and brought him close to her bosom.

She raised the fishing knife over his forehead.

Close to his eyes. "Life for life," she whispered.

Teresa screamed, "No!"

Her mother pulled Teresa behind her swiftly, and even with her hands confined, leapt forward.

Carly could see only blackness through the face cover. She had said her prayers, and held on to her daughter's wrist, even while the handcuffs had sawed against her own wrists. She had carefully followed her daughter up the trail, hoping that the police would come soon. Hoping that something would rescue them. Or something would help, some natural or supernatural agency. But no help had come.

When she heard Trey's voice, she thought he was near. But then, with Teresa's crying out, she knew that something was happening. Something bad.

Then she heard a bleating sound from Mark.

So she lunged in the direction of Agnes Hatcher's voice, keeping Teresa behind her. She had to make sure that nothing happened to her children.

What she felt when she lunged was a cold blade digging deep into her rib cage.

* * *

Agnes drew the knife out. "You bitch! You damned bitch!"

Teresa lay beside her mother. With her free hand she tore off the face cover. She looked at her mother's eyes. They were closed.

Don't be dead, Mommy. Please, don't be dead.

Ignoring the psycho woman who knelt over her with the knife, Teresa used her hands and teeth to tear off the rag tied around her mother's mouth. "She has to breathe! You're killing her!" Teresa said, turning to look at the psycho woman.

Agnes Hatcher held on to Mark. She shivered when she saw the anger in the girl's eyes. "Dying is good," Agnes said almost sweetly. "Hurting is good. It shows who you are on the inside."

Suddenly Mark began crying. He tugged at the handcuff, but was held fast in Agnes's arms. She kissed the top of his head. "Don't worry, little one. I'll show you where your mother lived. Not in her heart. Not like you. She lived in the lower part of her body. She lived where she created you."

Agnes traced the knife down Carly's body, down her stomach.

She raised the knife slightly.

"She lived where all whores live," Agnes said.

At that second, the sound of a gunshot rang through the caves.

Bats by the hundreds swept downward upon them. Teresa started screaming. She kept her face low, near her mother's. The bats brushed across her hair, tangling it.

The monk's chamber became black with bats as they dived down among the children. Agnes flailed the knife in the air as the bats slapped against her.

The knife dropped from her hand to the hard-packed dirt.

When the bats had cleared, Agnes lay in a heap across Carly's body.

The shadow of a man stood at the entrance to the circular room.

"Beloved," the man said.

CHAPTER 71

"Daddy!" Teresa wept, clutching her mother. "Daddy! Mommy's dead!"

But the man in the jagged doorway didn't look at her. He didn't seem like her father at all, because the expression he wore was different. He looked like someone else had crawled into his skin.

"It's taken me so long to come to you," he said, his arms outstretched.

CHAPTER 72

Agnes felt a doorway open within herself. He had found the key, finally. *He found the key!*

It was as if they were back in their nest, beneath the street in Whitechapel. It was like that last day. She was transformed—no longer in the body of the Hatcher woman, she was Agnes Graile, nineteen. Her Jack was there for her.

She went to his arms. "I'm sorry for what I did," she whispered, pressing her face against his neck. "I brought you all these lives so we could be together forever."

She smelled again the mildew and the coal. She kissed his neck. The scent of his soap was there—the scent of the gentleman surgeon.

"Leave them," he whispered. "They're nothing to us."

She smiled, nodding, and reached into her pocket for the key to the handcuffs. She smelled wonderful, as if she'd just taken a scented bath. It was as if her entire body chemistry had changed. There was no sea to her, no blood. Just the scent of flowers after a rain. She handed the small key to him. Trey took it and uncuffed the boy.

Then he hooked the empty handcuff around his own wrist. *If I can get her away from them. If I can just get her away from here.*

"Bound for all eternity," he said.

And then she felt the metal against the flesh of her breast.

Instinctively, she drew back from him. She saw the gun in his hand. "It's karma," she said dreamily. "What I did to you, you now do to me."

She reached for the gun, her hand closing over his.

Teresa wrapped her arms around her mother, weeping. She didn't understand why her father was acting so crazy.

Then she felt the breath on her cheek.

She drew back, looking at her mother.

Carly opened her eyes. She felt a pain below her chest. She tried to speak, but had some trouble. She tried to rise up, but had little energy.

Agnes squeezed the trigger of the gun—

Trey pulled it back and up, not wanting to kill her—

The bullet grazed Hatcher's shoulder—

Agnes knocked Trey backward with all her weight. It was as if she had the strength of several strong men.

He felt his knees buckle, and the wind was knocked out of him.

He fell to the floor, unconscious.

Agnes leaned over him. "I didn't mean to," she said, "It was the locket. I didn't mean to . . . the oven . . ."

Trey, waking, hearing her babbling about "locket" and "oven," realized that his act as her beloved Jack had sent her mind back to her repressed memory. He drifted in and out of consciousness for a few moments, had the hallucination that he was inside some dark cold metal closet and could hear rain outside.

As the rain spattered the streets and leaked into the basement, Agnes opened the small locket and saw the lock of dark hair and the woman's picture. It was some society woman. Jack had betrayed her.

He was there, hiding in the oven so that the police would not find him if they searched their nest. He was hiding behind rags and coal.

She felt the blood boil within her.

How could he betray her like that? They had sworn eternal devotion! They had mixed their blood with the blood of others—they were bound together for all time and eternity . . .

She soaked more rags in oil.

When she had several such rags, she opened the oven door slightly. She held the oil lamp up. In the light from the lamp she saw his eyes. He looked at her with love. She knew it was not meant for her. She was just a whore. She was just the street rag he had worn for a period of time. This other woman in the locket—she was the one he loved.

"Are they gone?" he whispered.

She answered him with fire.

Carly whispered to Teresa, "The knife."

Teresa stretched as far as she could to reach the fishing knife that had fallen in the dirt.

She said to Mark, "Marky! Help . . . Mommy needs help . . ." She pointed toward the knife, which was just a few feet from him.

Mark took a step toward the fishing knife.

It lay in the dirt, its metal shining red in the unholy light from the flares.

The images of Jesus on the cross seemed to dance in the flickering glow.

Trey came to full consciousness. He reached for the gun, but it wasn't near him.

Agnes, cuffed to him, dragged him up to his feet.

"I had to do it," she said, tears streaming down a face that still looked like a tigress ready to spring. She held the gun in her hand. "I had to. You were going to run off with her. You were going to forsake me. I couldn't let you. I knew it was the flesh that drew you. I knew that. I did it for us. So our love would not be tainted . . ."

She pointed the gun toward Carly. She drew Trey toward his wife and children. The handcuffs chafed his wrist. "When she dies, you'll understand."

"I do understand," Trey said. "And I love you."

A glimmer of hope sparkled in Agnes Hatcher's eyes.

For the first time since he'd been in his twenties, Trey thought she looked human. She was no longer the Gorgon or the Surgeon, but a much-abused girl who had not been allowed to fully develop. She looked like the most pitiable creature on the face of the earth. In a moment he remembered her life: the torture as a young girl, the rape, the darkness that was forced to blossom within her mind.

"If you love me, you'll watch her die," Agnes said. She aimed the gun for Carly's face.

Carly's eyes grew wide with terror.

Trey brought his free hand to Agnes Hatcher's face. He turned it toward his own. He kissed her strongly, passionately. "It's me. It's Jack," he said. Then he took the gun from her hand. "Let me murder the bitch."

Carly whispered, "Trey?"

"Shut up!" he yelled at her. Then, softly, to Agnes, "We can always be together now."

"Do you forgive me?"

"For what?"

Her mood suddenly changed. She wasn't buying the act. She went for the gun. "You'll know when I kill the bitch. Your eyes'll be opened."

Using all the strength he could muster, Trey jerked the handcuff. The gun dropped without firing. He and Agnes fell to the floor of the chamber. He groaned as he felt her knee connect with his groin, hard. She ground her knee into him there. He retched, and jabbed his elbow into her stomach.

She scratched at him blindly, as if fighting for her life. He punched her as hard as he could in the face. She bit down hard on his neck, drawing blood. They wrestled to the well—the rim of rocks at its edge keeping them from falling over. She managed to bring him down. She rolled on top of him and put her face close to his.

She foamed at the mouth. It was like having a bobcat sitting on top of him, small but strong and mean. "I'll make it right,'' she spat at him. ''It's not your fault.'' Through the wild look on her face, he saw into her eyes. She was a child there, they were swirls of colors, and she was lost within them. It was like watching someone where half their soul was at war with the other half. ''It's not your fault. It's 'cause of me, what I did. That night.''

And then a calm came over her. She half smiled. ''I know you love me. I know I was wrong.''

Her strength seemed to mellow, and she was no longer a heavy weight bearing down upon him, but light. He felt he could push her off.

He was about to do just that.

And then, as if fulfilling some destiny, she rolled over the edge of the chasm.

CHAPTER 73

Trey held on to one of the stone markers at the edge of the great well with his free arm. The handcuff with Agnes's weight pulling on it sliced into his wrist like a razor. If he tried, he could pull her up. He could save her. All his training had been to save and help and understand. But this woman was a monster. This woman had stabbed his wife in her rib. This woman would've tortured and killed his family. If he raised her up from the pit, even if he could, she would tear into him like a lion. But something within him still believed that she could be saved. That something in that monster soul could be salvaged.

Carly crawled slowly, snakelike, to the edge of the precipice. Teresa crawled along with her, still hand-cuffed to her.

Carly gripped Trey's arm where the handcuff was cutting into his wrist.

Agnes, dangling, but holding on, too, to what she

could of the walls of the natural well. "Jack," she whispered, "please, help me. I love you."

Then she tugged harder on the handcuff, kicking out from the wall. She didn't want help being brought up to safety.

She wanted to bring Trey over the edge with her.

CHAPTER 74

Carly held the fishing knife up in her free hand and brought it down. She hacked at Agnes Hatcher's wrist, cutting deep into her flesh.

Carly sawed with the knife until Agnes's small hand, bloody and torn, slipped loose from the cuff.

CHAPTER 75

Agnes Hatcher dropped into the darkness of the pit.

Trey heard the echo as she landed, and it sounded as if her spinal cord snapped.

CHAPTER 76

Trey held his wife and children as close to himself as he could get them. He tore his shirt off and wrapped it around Carly's side to help stop the wound up. He wanted to drown in the feeling of their skin, their smell, their sound, their taste as he kissed Mark's forehead and Teresa's cheek. He held his wife the longest, and they cried.

When he felt the strength, he helped Carly up. "Maybe you should go get help," she said.

"No," he said. "We'll make it back to the boat. I'm not going to leave you."

Carly was feeling weak, but she leaned against him as they walked back down the winding path of the cavern. Teresa held Mark's hand, but kept one hand on her father's back as he walked, just to make sure he was there.

When they came to the lower exit from the caverns,

they saw that the water had risen. The boats were gone, washed out with the tide.

"So, what now? An earthquake?" Carly asked, keeping her sense of humor intact.

Trey held up the flare. He set Carly down at the edge of the path. He instructed Mark and Teresa to stay with her.

Trey Campbell walked out into the dark sea, flare held high.

The water reached his chest, and he found a rock to climb on to.

He waved the flare back and forth, trusting that someone would see it and send help.

Within an hour he saw the lights of another boat. As it got closer, he saw that it was an old-fashioned fishing trawler. A man on board waved a lantern, and Trey shouted, waving the flare faster until it seemed like he'd painted the sky red with it.

CHAPTER 77

She heard him. The shout. Like a cry of joy.

Agnes Hatcher lay on a slanting rock shelf of the monk's well. The smells all around her were of sea anemone and urchin, and dead fish. The water was gently lapping at her back where it had risen with the tide. She would drown, or die from the fall. Or she would live and starve, too weak to call out for help—and then die slowly in several days. It didn't matter to her.

She stared up the sheer wall to the white chalk of the cavern, which seemed to glow in the dark. A memory came to her, not of a basement in Whitechapel, or of the man who had taken her from the gas station rest room.

She was ten, and at her parents' house. It was her birthday, and her father was taking her to the park to ride the ponies.

The memory was brief but intense: like a birthday candle just before it was blown out.

Her small hand within her father's larger hand.

Warmth.

She could not move, no matter how hard she tried. She felt the blood pulsing from her wrist.

It was like being in that room again at Darden.

Restrained.

But the cloth was off her face. She could see. At least she could still see.

Sight was its own kind of freedom.

Her lungs hurt, and breathing was difficult. All her energy went into each breath.

Minutes later she heard the rush of water as it flooded the well-like chamber.

The salt stung the stab wounds in her wrist. But pain was distant, like the crashing waves outside the caverns.

Death was like going home. It had to take you in when there was nowhere else to go.

She was going home, finally. After all this time.

She awaited, patiently, the next incarnation.

It came to her, not as the sea rushing over her face, nor as the blood drained from her body, but as a cloak of fire in her mind.

EPILOGUE

After the old fisherman had located them and brought them back to town, and after Carly got patched up at a local clinic, they had spent the morning at the police station, giving their statements to Oscar Arboles. They had spent the afternoon sleeping at the Breakers hotel. He had slept in a bed wrapped around his wife; his children in cots in the same room. He didn't know how long a time would pass until he would allow them out of his sight. Trey had been awakened by the sounds of the firecrackers.

"Oh," he said, waking Carly. "It's the Fourth."

She rubbed her eyes. He kissed her several times before he could bring himself to get out of bed.

"Would it be foolish to take the kids to see the fireworks?" Carly asked. She was feeling better. "I mean, after all we've been through?"

"We're on vacation," Trey answered. "Why not?"

* * *

Avalon had set a platformlike barge out in the bay. The local fire department was shooting the fireworks off from there. Yachts and sloops of all sizes speckled the horizon. A band was playing John Philip Sousa marches from the docks. The beach was a sea of sparklers as children waved them and small flags around. Tourists had packed the place in twenty-four hours.

That night Trey sat out in another rented Bayrunner Westcoaster, holding Carly, while Mark and Teresa were amazed by the night fireworks.

The last rocket was launched and sprayed a rainbow of color across the night.

For a second Trey felt something tugging within him.

"Something wrong?" Carly asked, noticing his change of expression.

He didn't want to say what he felt. He said, "Just happy we made it through."

"They'll find her body," Carly said. "No one could survive that fall. Not even her."

Trey Campbell returned his attention to the falling sparkles, and to the renewed joy in his children's faces.

But he felt it again.

Within him.

She's gone.

He thought he'd heard her voice whisper to him, *Beloved!*

Trey imagined a stone alley, and a shivering young girl standing in its corner. She watched the basement of an adjoining tenement rage with fire. As the flames shot up through the night, the girl moved closer to the fire, as if looking for something.

"Are you there?" she asked the fire. "Jack?"

Trey tried to warn her away, but the girl pulled her cloak closer around her shoulders. She moved toward the burning building. She lifted a grate that was red from heat. The flesh of her fingers burned against it. As the tongues of fire shot up from below, the girl descended into the burning room.

Trey thought he saw them clutch at each other as if they were the only souls in the world. Clutch and claw and embrace as the flames engulfed them.

He watched the sky brighten with one last shattering spray of light. For a moment, it illuminated the heavens. And then the sky was dark, a mystery.

Trey Campbell wondered if, somewhere safe, she would be reborn.